"I do not wish to see you make a fool of yourself, the boy is years younger than you!" Merriot said...

"Make a fool of myself?" Eleanor repeated incredulously. "Is it possible you believe I am in love with that silly young man? You are insufferable!"

"Really? Then perhaps I am wrong, perhaps you regard him as an eligible *parti*. I am sorry to disillusion you, my dear. The title is quite valueless," he told her sarcastically.

"Oh!" gasped Eleanor. "Oh, I should like to hit you for that."

Merriot strode across the room and jerked her roughly into his arms. "Eleanor, Eleanor!" he muttered huskily and crushed her mouth under his . . .

Second Chance at Love™
REGENCY

THE CAUTIOUS HEART
PHILIPPA HEYWOOD

A JOVE BOOK

First Jove edition published August 1981

First printing

"Second Chance at Love" and the butterfly emblem are
trademarks belonging to Jove Publications, Inc.

Printed in the United States of America

Jove books are published by Jove Publications, Inc.,
200 Madison Avenue, New York, NY 10016

chapter 1

The morning room in Hawthorne Place was a spacious, elegant apartment, furnished in the latest mode. Unfortunately, it was also extremely drafty and its present occupants, two damsels of some seventeen summers, were obliged to huddle close to the cheerful fire in order to keep their teeth from chattering. One was sitting in front of an enormous embroidery frame. The other, a plump, pretty chit, had a volume of sermons open upon her lap. Neither lady was engaged in these admirable pursuits, however; instead they were enjoying a comfortable gossip.

"You do not know how fortunate you are to have an aunt like dear Miss Portland living in the house, Emily," said Harriet in envious tones. "I am sure she is the most understanding grownup I have ever met, for she does not prose on and on or lecture one. She is so elegant, too. I wonder why it is that she never married. I should think she must have had lots of offers, don't you?"

Emily smiled mysteriously and lowered her voice to a conspiratorial whisper. "Well, I know all about it and I will tell you if you will swear upon your honor never to breathe a word of it. Mama told me in the strictest confidence, and she said that I must never, never mention it, especially to Papa or Aunt Eleanor."

Harriet nodded her mousy curls vigorously, her eyes sparkling behind the spectacles that gave her piquant face an owlish appearance. "I will never say a word, I promise. Not even to Mama!"

"Very well then. It was the most dreadful scandal!" announced Emily in thrilling accents. "When she was in her first Season, Aunt Eleanor fell madly in love with a gentleman. I believe he was a Viscount, but Mama would not tell me which one. Anyway, the truly dreadful part is that he was married already!"

"Oh!" gasped Harriet, pleasurably shocked.

"And," Emily went on quickly, sure of her listener's interest, "it seems the gentleman was just as much in love with her as she was with him! He persuaded her to run away with him! Mama does not know that I have heard this part, for Betty told me. They were on their way to the continent and there was an accident to the carriage. They were obliged to spend the night together, quite alone and... in the same room!"

This disclosure proved too much for Harriet, who blushed and wished very much that Emily had never told her the story. She had thought Emily's Aunt Eleanor quite the nicest lady she knew and this revelation distressed her a great deal.

"What happened?" she asked anxiously. "She did not have a . . . I mean she was not . . . ?"

"Good gracious, no! At least I do not think so. In any event Grandpapa went after them and brought Aunt Eleanor home in disgrace. It is a terrible shame I think, for from that day to this she has never gone beyond the village boundary, not even to an Assembly at York. Papa never mentions it of course, and neither does she, but the tale is that Grandpapa fought the Viscount. And it was soon afterward that Grandpapa had his stroke."

Harriet sat in silence, digesting this unhappy tale. How poor Miss Portland must have blamed herself for her father's illness! What she must have suffered! Yet she seemed happy and cheerful enough. Of course years had passed, but still Harriet was quite sure that she herself would *never* recover if anything half so tragic were to happen to her.

At that moment the door opened and the subject of their

discussion entered the room. No one who overheard the girls' chatter would have recognized the poor unfortunate lady of Emily's story. The woman who entered the room was not only graceful and stylishly dressed, but she looked not a day over twenty-five. In fact she was seven-and-twenty and, although she had certainly lost the youthful bloom she had once possessed, there were many who considered her more beautiful than she had ever been. True, the dimpled softness of her cheeks had gone, but now the ivory skin was stretched taut across the delicately molded bones of her face. Her smiling gray eyes held an expression of calm amusement as though she surveyed the world around her with tolerance and would not take it very seriously. And she certainly hadn't lost interest in her appearance. Her gown of lavender kerseymere, so delicate a wool and so beautifully woven, was demure enough for country wear, yet fashioned in such a way as to flatter her magnificent figure. There was nothing remotely demure, however, about the plentiful red-gold ringlets which clustered about her head.

She surveyed the two girls for a moment as she stood in the doorway, then she moved gracefully to the fireplace, holding out slender, ringless fingers to the blaze.

"Well, *mes petites*, are you having a comfortable coze?" she asked with a quizzical lift of the eyebrow. Probably Harriet's blushes and guilty looks gave her a tolerably accurate idea of the subject the girls had been discussing.

"Oh, yes, Aunt Eleanor," responded Emily, brazening it out. "We were talking about going to London this Season, if Papa will only consent to let me. Then Mr. Milton will allow Harriet to come too, and we will have a perfectly splendid time together!"

Her aunt smiled in tender amusement. "I hope very much you will be able to go and have your 'splendid time,' my dear, for I think that you are in the greatest danger of being spoiled to death if you remain here. The whole County makes a pet of you. It is not at all good for you."

Emily jumped up and flung her arms around her aunt. "I think you spoil me just as badly as everyone else, dearest, kindest Aunt Eleanor. I love you very, very much!"

Eleanor could not but kiss the smiling young face for there was no doubt that Emily was a dear sweet child and quite ridiculously pretty for all her plumpness. However, she was only too aware that her niece could be difficult for she had experienced her sudden tantrums. She wished she were in a position to give the girl's mother some advice on handling her, but she knew that Maria would never listen. Lady Portland couldn't be brought to tolerate her sister-in-law and bitterly resented her presence at Hawthorne Place. Eleanor had long been aware of her sister-in-law's attitude. While once it had distressed her, she now ignored the dislike which sprang, she knew, not from moral indignation, but merely from envy and malice. Maria, always jealous of her husband's affection for his sister, was even more resentful of Emily's adoration of her youthful aunt.

These reflections were interrupted by Emily, who had thrust a copy of *La Belle Assemblée* under her nose, demanding her opinion of a gown depicted there. Eleanor turned her energies to the demanding task of convincing the girl that to appear abroad in a dress more suited to a matron of forty than a debutante could not be thought to her advantage.

Meanwhile Harriet had recovered her countenance and, when called upon to second her friend, felt obliged instead to side with Miss Portland.

"No, Emmy, it would not become you at all," she told her pouting friend firmly. "All that tucking and frilling, why it would make you look so fat!"

Eleanor, who would never have said such a tactless thing, was surprised at the instant effect these words had upon her volatile niece. No more was heard of the gown's many perfections. She regarded Harriet Milton with approval. While Emily had such a sensible little companion, there was no need to fear her high spirits would lead beyond the line of what was pleasing in a young girl. Moreover, Harriet had style, and though she was not nearly as pretty as her friend, she could upon occasion make Emily look quite commonplace. Thankfully, she did not consciously do so—Harriet's devotion to her old playmate was steadfast and usually quite uncritical.

Eleanor meanwhile had been turning the pages of the fashion journal and had come upon an illustration of a gown which she knew would become her niece admirably. It was a pretty, open robe of primrose sarsenet, worn over a satin slip.

"This is exactly the sort of thing you should wear," she advised, directing Emily's attention to the page.

Emily pulled a face. "Oh, Aunt, it would make me look like a schoolgirl!"

The three ladies were hotly debating the issue when the door opened once more and Lady Portland stalked into the room.

In her youth Maria Spencer had been pretty enough, very like her daughter, but an unhappy marriage and a naturally sour, joyless disposition had so worked upon her looks that all traces of former beauty had vanished. At five-and-thirty she was a hard-faced matron with little dignity and no style whatsoever.

"I am surprised to see you here, Eleanor," she remarked as she entered the room. "I had thought you had so many important things to do." Her tone was one of more than a little sarcasm, as Eleanor had earlier refused to run an errand into the village on the score of having letters to write.

"I have but this moment joined the girls," Eleanor responded with the calm good humor which so irritated Maria. "However, I am quite at your disposal now if there is anything I may do for you."

"No, no, I sent one of the maids out," answered her ladyship testily. "Emily, for goodness sake straighten your sash. You look the most complete hoyden. And I daresay you have not read one word of that excellent book I lent to you."

"Indeed I have, Mama," declared Emily unblushingly. "We were just now discussing one of Dr. Robertson's points. Were we not?"

Harriet nodded while Eleanor merely smiled, neither having the heart to betray Emily. Eleanor knew she shouldn't abet her niece in flouting her mama, but she thought her sister-in-law excessively foolish to expect the high-spirited girl to spend her time reading sermons.

Uncharacteristically, Lady Portland dropped the matter. She lowered herself rather painfully into an armchair and seemed content to listen to the others chatter for a while. It remained for Harriet, who for all her short-sightedness was an observant little thing, to first notice that something was wrong.

"Are you ill, Lady Portland?" she asked suddenly. "You look pale."

It was true. Lady Portland's usually florid countenance had turned quite white, and she seemed breathless. Eleanor regarded her with real concern.

"Maria, I will run to procure a cordial from Nurse. You look ready to faint!"

"No such thing, I am perfectly well," declared her ladyship. But even as she spoke she seemed racked with a sudden spasm of pain and clutched her breast before collapsing back into her chair in a deep swoon.

Always at her most efficient in a crisis, Eleanor had her sister-in-law conveyed to her chamber and divested of her garments in a remarkably short space of time.

The local doctor was of course immediately summoned. He arrived speedily, for the family members at Hawthorne Place were his most valued patients. Moreover, he was fond of them for he had brought two generations of them into the world.

Eleanor greeted the familiar figure with relief and took him immediately to Lady Portland. While he conducted his examination, she attempted to bring some order to the suddenly disrupted household. Why the collapse of a much-disliked mistress should have induced half the maidservants to succumb to hysterics, she was quite unable to fathom. She did her best to soothe them and to calm the corpulent chef whose main concern was that his well-prepared dinner would be spoiled. She had only just ascended from the nether regions when the doctor came down. His report was heartening as he indicated there was no immediate danger, then disheartening as he stated that Lady Portland had a heart condition which required the best of care—complete rest and no undue excitement.

It was just under two hours when Lord Portland arrived back from York to find his household in an uproar because of his wife's illness. A fine man, much liked in the neighborhood, he bore a strong resemblance to his sister. What had induced a good-looking, wealthy, and amiable young man to offer for Maria Spencer was something that none of his well-wishers had been able to fathom. The supposedly premature birth of Emily some six months later had enlightened them. And, if he had acted wrongly in seducing such a well-born damsel, he had certainly acted most honorably ever since. Any fondness he had felt for his wife had long ago disappeared, but he was a gentleman and naturally he wished to do everything he could to insure her welfare. There was no denying, however, that his wife's indisposition had come at a deucedly inconvenient time. The business that had taken him into York had been nothing less than the signing of a six-month lease for a house in Mayfair which he had taken for the Season. He had planned the whole thing as a delightful surprise for Emily. Not only was he loathe to disappoint her, he also had put down a large deposit upon the house which he was by no means anxious to forfeit. Of course, if Maria could not go, that was the end of their plans. A debutante must have a chaperone. Briefly, he considered hiring one but such women were invariably shabby-genteel and could not add to his daughter's consequence.

Just as he was occupied with these reflections, Eleanor, as usual serene and composed, passed by. And Lord Portland was struck by a brilliant idea! Eleanor would be the perfect chaperone. Emily already minded her far better than she did her mama, for she admired her aunt and wished to be like her. Of course the idea had to be given careful consideration—but after all, that old scandal had taken place over ten years ago. His sister was seven-and-twenty now. Surely people would have forgotten. The more he considered it, the better he liked the notion. Eleanor should go with Emily to London and chaperone her to all the *ton* parties. They would do very well after all!

Miss Portland did not see the matter in quite the same light when he put his idea to her over dinner.

"You must be mad, Peter, to think of such a thing. You know very well why I will never visit London again!"

"Damn it, girl, all that happened years ago. Who is going to remember it now?"

"I remember. I remember it, Peter, as though it were yesterday. Do you not understand? It is not the world I fear, nor scandal. It is myself. I do not trust myself to be near him again! Even to be in the same city would be a torment!"

Lord Portland stared at his sister in amazement. "You mean to say that after all these years you are still in love with the fellow?"

"Yes! No! Oh, I do not know! Don't you see, I dare not risk finding out. Peter, you above all people know what I went through. It has not been easy for me these past years. I have worked hard to regain a little peace and self-respect. I will not go back to suffering as I did. I am afraid to."

Lord Portland sighed and philosophically shrugged his broad shoulders. "Well, Eleanor, I will not press you if that is the way you feel. But think it over, my dear. Emily's happiness depends upon you for I dare not think of her disappointment if she is not able to have her Season!"

He departed the room, more seriously displeased with his sister than he had been in all the time that she had made her home with him. Chaperoning Emily seemed a very small favor to ask in return for the comfortable home he had provided the last ten years. Lord Portland began to feel most ill-used.

Eleanor was left to her own reflections, and agitated they were. For years she had deliberately closed her mind to thoughts of that mad springtime. Now they had been revived, and in spite of herself they flooded her memory like sunlight pouring into a dusty room.

She had been just seventeen, as excited and happy as Emily over the prospect of a London Season. She knew she was expected to find an eligible husband, but in her dreams this suitor was always as handsome and dashing as he was rich. When she arrived in town, however, none of the estimable men she encountered fulfilled her expectations . . . none until she met Viscount Lennox.

One bright morning, earlier than most of the *ton* were abroad, Eleanor was riding in the Park. She enjoyed the fresh cool breeze that fanned her cheeks and cleared her head, still heavy from the entertainment of the night before. All at once her pretty chestnut mare, too mettlesome for her inexperienced hands, took fright and bolted. She was quite unable to halt the terrified beast and certainly would have been thrown had not another rider been at hand to capture the animal and bring it to a halt. She was near to fainting, and the man lifted her from the saddle as easily as though she had been a child. She leaned against his chest, thankful for the security of his supporting arms. As his hold tightened, however, she became suddenly aware of the impropriety of her situation and broke away from him. Shyly, she lifted her glowing eyes to his face and expressed her thanks. He caught his breath as he gazed into her flowerlike countenance, and she stared incredulously into the most handsome face she had ever seen. She managed to stammer some foolish words of gratitude before her tardy groom arrived. The rider bowed in answer, remounted his own long-tailed gray, and trotted away.

The memory of the man's burning glance remained with her and would not be dismissed. She longed to see him again. And she did, a few days later, at an entertainment given by one of London's most fashionable hostesses.

Eleanor was waltzing with an agreeable young man when

she caught sight of him. Immediately she asked her partner
who he might be.

"Oh, that's Lennox, Viscount Lennox, you know. And I
think . . . Yes, that's Lady Lennox over there," had answered
her partner cheerfully.

"Lady Lennox?" she questioned.

"Yes, lucky devil. That's his wife, the ravishing creature
in green."

Eleanor gazed miserably upon a woman who seemed to her
envious eyes to be lovely beyond belief. From her shining
ebony ringlets to her dainty, elegantly-shod feet, she was the
epitome of everything Eleanor thought she wished to be. With
such a beautiful, sophisticated wife, how could she have been
so foolish as to think that he had regarded her with admiration?
No doubt he'd thought her an awkward schoolgirl.

Very sensibly Eleanor resolved to banish Lord Lennox from
her thoughts, and, if he did intrude upon her dreams, she could
not be held responsible for that! She was succeeding very well
in forgetting all about him when she was once more made
aware of him in a most dramatic way.

Although an innocent girl, she was by no means stupid, and
for some time she had been aware of constant rumors about
Lady Lennox. It seemed her husband's attentions were not
enough to satisfy her. She had an insatiable appetite for new
lovers, and, it was said, no one knew who was the father of
her son, least of all the lady herself. Eleanor had heard of such
women before but she always imagined them to be the kind
of loose females from the village whom her mother had aided
when they came up to the house with the fruits of their liaisons.
It had never occurred to her that a high-born and beautiful lady
could behave in such a way.

Attending a rather boring soirée one evening, Eleanor felt
so hot and tired she slipped away from the crowd and found
a comfortable seat in a secluded alcove. Exhausted by all the
late nights that had recently been her lot, she very soon fell
fast asleep in the dim recess.

She was awakened by the sound of voices. They were low,
but there was a passionate intensity in them that penetrated her
dreams.

A man was speaking, his voice so husky that she scarcely
could make out his words. "Alyce, do not play with me. You

brought me here . . . Alyce, I want you, I adore you . . . damn it, you know you want it too!"

"Do I?" answered a woman's voice, lightly teasing. "I wonder."

"Let me show you what love can really be like, Alyce. What does that dull stick, your husband, know? Does he touch you like this? Does he kiss you like this?"

In answer, Alyce sighed. For some time Eleanor was made excessively uncomfortable by being forced to listen to sounds which she was too innocent to recognize, but which nonetheless made her feel hot and embarrassed. She desperately wanted to leave. But how could she? It would have been more than awkward to appear suddenly out of the shadows to interrupt these people in whatever it was they were doing.

She heard another voice, one she recognized instantly.

"So Alyce, even here you cannot restrain yourself. Must you behave like a bitch in heat even in the houses of our friends?"

There was the sound of a slap followed by a rather hysterical laugh from the woman. "Come, Devereaux, let us leave my husband to his moralizing. Do not worry, he is not going to challenge you. Are you, my brave husband?"

"My dear, if I went out at dawn to meet every one of your lovers, I should never get a decent night's sleep."

The woman laughed again and then silence reigned for some time. Eleanor remained in her hiding place for, before emerging, she wished to make quite sure that everyone concerned had left. When she did rise, however, it was to realize that she was not alone after all. Lord Lennox was sitting on the chaise longue so recently occupied by his wife. His head was buried in his hands, and he had a defeated air which instantly awoke in Eleanor a desire to comfort him.

"Sir," she murmured hesitantly. "Sir, please do not be so unhappy. I cannot bear to see you so."

His head jerked up at the sound of her voice. "You!" he cried. "How long have you been here?"

"All the time," she admitted shamefacedly. "I did not know how to get away."

"So now you, too, know the truth. Look at me, an object of derision to every wag in town. Cuckolded by more men than even she can count. What a spectacle!"

Agonized by his misery she comforted him in the only way

she could. Kneeling at his side she put her soft young arms about him and laid her cheek against his.

"Dear sir, no one laughs at you. Everyone admires you for the way you stand by your wife. Indeed it is true, for I have heard people say it."

He smiled down into her anxious face. "What a dear little liar you are." He bent his head and pressed his lips against hers. They trembled softly under his, but she did not turn away from him. That kiss set the seal upon their love, a love that was to bring Eleanor ruin and disgrace.

The sound of Emily's voice calling to her jerked Eleanor back into the present. Firmly she pulled herself together and when Emily burst into the chamber she noticed nothing amiss with her aunt.

"Aunt Eleanor, dearest Aunt, Papa has such a famous scheme! Has he told you? We are to go to London after all. You and I and Harriet. Oh, what fun we shall have! I shall have a much nicer time with you than with poor Mama. Are you not excited?"

Miss Portland was furious with her brother for his treachery. How could she tell his boisterous child she would not go? She must be told, however. Anything was better than facing Lennox once more!

"Your Papa should not have mentioned this, Emily. He does not have my consent. Indeed, I told him directly that it is not to be thought of."

"But why not?" she wailed miserably. "We would have such *fun!*"

"Fun! Fun for you, Emily, no doubt, but purgatory for me!" Eleanor burst out passionately. "I cannot do it! I will not do it! Do not mention this to me again. Do you understand, Emily? I wish to hear no more about it."

Emily shrank from her aunt. She had never seen her so moved, and it frightened her.

"Very well, Aunt," she murmured contritely. "I'm sorry if I angered you."

Eleanor caught the unhappy child in her arms. "Not you, sweetheart. It is not you that I am angry with."

"Then who?" demanded Emily, ungrammatically.

"With myself!"

Emily wriggled free and pulled a face.

"I do not see any sense in that. I should never be angry with myself when there are quite enough people to be horrid to me as it is!"

Eleanor laughed. "I hope, my little one, that you never have cause to be angry at yourself as I have. Leave me for a while, my dear. I have much to do."

Emily departed with rather less noise than she had arrived, leaving Eleanor once more to drift into the past and dream of those stolen moments of happiness with Lennox.

They had often met in secluded corners of the less fashionable parks. Eleanor would slip out of the house at dusk and hurry nervously through the streets until she came to the gateway where his servant would be waiting to escort her to their trysting place.

She would sit happily within the circle of his arms while he talked to her of his life, of the son he adored yet doubted was his own, and most often, of the misery his wife caused him. He had been madly in love with the beautiful creature when he married her, but later realized she had married him only because she wished to be a Viscountess. She scorned his lovemaking and even at that time she had many lovers with whom she could compare him. He believed now it was a sickness with her, but that did not make her constant infidelity any easier to bear. But when Eleanor in her innocence asked him why he did not leave his wife, he was shocked.

"My sweet, you do not understand. Such a thing is not possible in our world. I cannot divorce Alyce. It is not honorable."

"Is this honorable?" she asked. "Is it right to meet like this, sneaking about in the darkness as though we were ashamed of loving one another? Do you really think it right?"

"Eleanor darling, all I know is that I love you. I cannot lose you now."

As always she succumbed to his passion and his kisses. She would go on meeting him a little longer. In truth, she would have found it hard to give up their times together for he awakened her to a passion which threatened to dominate her. When she lay in his arms she felt more truly alive than ever before.

Even so, she did not commit the final act that would make her his mistress. Such a thing was unthinkable to a gently-bred young girl. She felt it wrong to enjoy his embraces as much as she did. As for the feelings he had aroused when once he had caressed her breasts—she dared not think of them for she would flush hotly and find herself shaking. She had longed to give herself to him completely. She had run from him and refused to see him for days until loneliness and his unhappiness had brought her back to his arms. He was careful never to alarm her again.

It was the news that Lady Lennox was pregnant once more that brought matters to a head. He broke it to her one evening as they sat together upon a bench. He was gently stroking her hair while with the other hand he played with the fingers of her hand. She accepted the news with equanimity, but stiffened when he continued: "And the devil of it is I do not know if this one is mine."

She drew her hand from his and sat up abruptly. "What do you mean? How could the baby be yours?"

He looked at her uncomprehendingly. "It may be," he answered. "Who knows? I doubt if she does."

"But it *may* be? You mean that you still... That all this time while you have been saying you love me you have been making love to *her*? You told me you hated her!"

"You do not understand, Eleanor. A man must have some release. My wife is a very beautiful woman, and she can be damnably seductive when it suits her. What we do together has nothing to do with love. Not the kind of love I have for you."

"I thought you really loved me, but I see I was wrong. How could I have been so stupid? I will not go on like this! I cannot share you with that horrid woman. I feel dirtied and used. I never wish to see you again, Richard. Never!"

He begged her to stay, to listen to him. She would not. She would not share him with his wife. He must choose between them.

They did not meet for several weeks. She ignored the notes he sent. One night when she found herself seated next to him at a dinner party, she turned a white shoulder and talked animatedly to her other neighbor. Such treatment had its effect. Finding her alone during that evening he fell upon his knees before her and begged her to run away with him. They would go to Italy, go anywhere, so long as they could be together. Carried away by her infatuation, Eleanor agreed.

It was not difficult to get away because Eleanor's papa was indulgent and did not chaperone her too strictly. She was able to slip out of the house as she had a dozen times before, but this time her lover was waiting for her with a chaise and four.

As she settled back against the cushions Eleanor was breathlessly happy and quite unafraid. To a girl of seventeen in love with the hero of her dreams the claims of family and respectability seemed small. She was quite sincerely happy to give up everything she knew, the comfortable world she inhabited, just to be with Lennox.

The accident to the chaise as they neared Dover was annoying, but that practical streak in Eleanor which often disconcerted her lover asserted itself. What did it matter if she were to become a fallen woman on this side of the Channel rather than upon foreign soil? She gave a giggle, surprised at her own daring—the country girl had become heady with her lover's commitment.

Fortunately, they had been close to a small inn when the accident had taken place and were able to put up for the night without difficulty. Naturally, Lennox told the innkeeper that the lady accompanying him was his wife and any doubts that worthy may have harbored he kept to himself.

Lennox led her upstairs, taking her hand, and to his surprise, it was his hand that shook, not hers. As they entered the bedchamber he whispered, "My sweet, will you trust yourself to me?"

She smiled at him with breathtaking sweetness. "Richard, I love you so much, of course I trust you." She held out her arms to him. "You see, my darling, I want you too, just as much as you want me."

Too shy to undress before him, she banished him to the hall. But when she had slipped out of her fashionable gown and, with some blushing, divested herself of her undergarments, she caught a glimpse of herself, slim and white, in the mirror. The sight gave her courage and she called to him. "I am ready now, Richard. Come in, my love."

She could remember every detail of that night. The warmth of another body against her own, the touch of his lips, the feel of his hands gently caressing her. Then the sudden, unexpected pain, blotting out every feeling of pleasure. Later he had wooed her once more, and this time there had been no pain—only a pleasure so intense that she thought she would die of it. They had slept in each other's arms, satiated and at peace.

The next morning the idyll was over. They had been pursued. Who had betrayed her she never knew, but her father arrived with two stout men. She was taken screaming from the inn and flung helpless into a coach. The last thing she saw through her tears was her father striking Lennox across the mouth with his heavy leather glove.

She learned later that they had met and that Lennox had fired in the air, admitting his guilt. Fortunately, her father was too poor a marksman to injure his opponent fatally, although he inflicted a severe wound.

Eleanor had been soundly whipped and brought home in disgrace. For months she had expected Lennox to come for her. Every carriage that arrived at the house raised her hopes, only to be dashed. She received no letters, and from the day she left him to the present she had received no word. It had been long before she could support life again, but gradually she had regained her serenity and even, after long years, a degree of cheerfulness. Was this hard-won peace to be risked for the sake of gratifying a petulant child? No! No! Nothing would induce her to go to London. Nothing would ever make her see Lennox once more.

chapter 2

It should not be supposed that Eleanor's decision was accepted as final by her family. They attacked her separately and together with tears, cajolery, and threats, but to no avail. Much as she loved her niece, Miss Portland could be firm when she believed herself to be right as now she did. Surprisingly, her only supporter proved to be her sister-in-law who, having recovered sufficiently to be once more laying down the law to the rest of the household, stated that she had not suspected Eleanor of having so much proper feeling. By this stage, Eleanor was so harassed that even this moderate praise was welcome.

One morning as she endeavored with little success to turn her mind from the projected visit, Lord Portland came into the sitting room. He bent and kissed her cheek.

"Eleanor, Sir Charles Warrington and I have been having a little talk. I know I may speak plainly to you for you are a sensible girl. Young Warrington is hanging out for a wife and there is no reason why, if he should take a fancy to her, that our little Emily should not be Lady Warrington some day."

"I see," remarked Eleanor. "It is to be hoped that Emily will be allowed some say in the matter, Peter."

"Of course, of course. What do you take me for? In any event, we have decided to let the young people become acquainted without making too much of a point of it. We have determined that a meeting at a Public Assembly would be the best place to make a start."

Eleanor looked a little puzzled. "What has this to do with me, Peter?" she questioned.

"Well, my dear, as poor Maria is still quite done up, I must ask you to chaperone Emily to this ball."

"Oh! Oh, I see!" exclaimed Eleanor. "But will not Lady Warrington do so?"

"My good girl, I have just explained that we wish to avoid any appearance of particularity. The meeting must seem simply a chance one. Emily cannot go without a lady to attend her. Will you go with her? To please me."

It was ten years since Eleanor had attended even the most modest party and her first reaction was to recoil from the prospect. Yet as she considered the matter she could not but admit that the small outing would make a welcome change in her monotonous existence. No, upon reflection she was by no means averse to the idea.

"Very well, Peter," she answered him after a moment's pause. "Yes, since you ask it of me, I should like to go."

"That's my good girl." He smiled before giving her a brotherly hug. "I knew you would not let me down in this. Why, if Emily can catch George Warrington, then she will have a house in London and as many Seasons as she could desire. You will be spared from accompanying her, and it will not cost me a penny!"

He was about to leave the room when Eleanor thought of a most important point.

"Stay a moment, Peter!"

He turned, halfway to the door. "Yes?"

"Do you not think that as Emily is to appear in Society for the first time a new gown would be in order?"

"Oh, certainly, certainly. Whatever you think best, my dear. Do not consider the cost."

Eleanor coughed discreetly. "As it happens, Peter, I have not a rag fit to wear either. All my ball dresses are fashioned at least ten years behind the mode."

He laughed. "I see what it is. Very well, you shall both have smart new gowns, and I for one shall not be at all surprised if you stand up for as many sets as Emily. Although you do not realize it, Eleanor, you are still a very personable woman. Very personable indeed!"

Upon this remark he departed, leaving his sister in a much more cheerful frame of mind than she had enjoyed for some time. It occurred to her that her life had become so stagnant that even the very ordinary pleasure of a public ball had the power to excite her—she who had once waltzed at Almacks. She gave a little sigh, picked up a dog-eared copy of *La Belle Assemblée* left by Emily, and began to flip through the pages.

Emily, when told of the treat in store, was every bit as delighted as her aunt and a good deal more noisy.

"Oh, Papa!" she cried, throwing herself upon his chest. "How absolutely lovely!"

He smiled down at her and patted her curls. "Well, you must thank your kind aunt and repay her by being a good girl. You must not tease her anymore about that wretched trip to London. She has been made unhappy, and I am sorry for it. So let us hear no more about it. Do you understand me, Emily?"

"Yes, Papa," she answered docilely, too thrilled by the immediate prospect to repine over anything lost in the future.

Emily and Eleanor passed many pleasant afternoons studying the fashion plates and thoroughly discussing the merits of the various gowns depicted therein. They then traveled to the nearby market town of Pudsley to visit the one fashionable modiste the little town could boast. Fortunately, they found themselves able to command services of Madame Le Tour, an elderly emigrée who had settled in Pudsley after fleeing the ravages of the French Revolution. Once gownmaker for the ladies of the brilliant French Court, she was now content to dress the wives and daughters of local mill owners.

Her taste was impeccable, and she saw in a moment that her new client would look magnificent in a gown of vivid green satin. With that glorious coppery hair and translucent skin Eleanor could carry off the color as few women could. The gown was fashioned in emerald satin with an overdress of pale gold gauze. It was cut low as was the mode and displayed Eleanor's figure to great advantage. A short train indicated that she had no intention of dancing. It was a daring gown, and when she tried it on for the first time in front of the mirror in her own chamber Eleanor was a little nervous at the prospect of appearing in it. But then it was so very becoming, and she was tired of being always proper and sensible. She wanted to be beautiful again, to be admired once more. Surely there was some other life possible for her than this gradual decline into spinsterhood. For the first time in years she felt that perhaps there might be.

Just as the sun descended behind the distant hills, Eleanor and Emily entered Lord Portland's luxurious carriage. Some hour and a half later, they arrived at the Assembly Rooms in York. The roads were still extremely muddied from a heavy fall of snow earlier that month, or they would have completed the journey in under an hour with ease, the coachman assured them.

The rooms, spacious and well-proportioned, were full to overflowing when the ladies entered. And though the building boasted no architectural conceits such as the octagonal card room in the Bath Assembly Rooms the citizens of York were justifiably proud of their new edifice.

Lord Portland being a prominent man in the area, the majority of the assembled company was familiar to the ladies. Mr. Fenwick, the Master of Ceremonies, came forward to greet them as honored guests and presented each with a dance program. This Eleanor refused. She did not wish to dance and did not anticipate that she would receive any offers to do so. They made their way with some difficulty across the room to the seats reserved for the local gentry where Eleanor found herself seated by several ladies whom she had known since childhood.

"My dear," began one of these ladies immediately, "I cannot tell you how pleased I am to see you here. I always did think it ridiculous that you should lock yourself away. I hope this marks the end to such silly behavior!"

Eleanor was too well acquainted with Mrs. Derwent to be offended by this forthright speech which, she believed, sprang from the kindest motives. The other ladies were nodding and smiling at her so she concluded they had agreed together that it was time to forget the shocking scandal in her past. She could remember a period not so long ago when these same women had been far from cordial, but she did not really blame them. Emily was a great favorite, a pet to these ladies, but the girl had little time to enjoy their attentions before her hand was claimed for a set which was forming.

Eleanor felt a trifle guilty in allowing Emily to dance with the young gentleman presented to her by Mr. Fenwick. She knew her brother would have wanted her to keep Emily by her side until George Warrington made his appearance. Her pride revolted on her niece's behalf. Mr. Warrington was not to think that he had only to throw down his handkerchief and Emily would be ready to pick it up!

As she watched the young couple moving gracefully down the dance line she became aware of a sudden excitement among her companions. They were all chattering loudly, their attention directed at someone who had just entered the ballroom.

"That's him," one lady whispered to another. "Fancy his bothering to attend our little Assembly. They say he has twenty thousand a year and very likely more. I wonder if he will ask any of our girls to dance!"

"I certainly hope he will *not*," said another matron reprovingly. "His reputation precludes his standing up with any respectable girl, and so I shall tell him if he should ask for Melissa's hand." The young lady in question, a rabbit-faced girl with a pasty complexion, looked a little wistful, but made no answer.

Eleanor could be nothing but interested, of course. In the doorway she saw a tall man surrounded by a group of persons with whom he seemed very much bored. Her first thought was that he was one of the most striking men she had ever seen. There was something arrogant and faintly dangerous about him even as he stood exchanging civilities. While tall enough to dwarf most of the men around him, he carried himself with careless grace. His thick black locks—brushed into the "Brutus" style Mr. Brummell had made so popular—framed a face whose features were good, but whose expression was hard and faintly mocking. Intrigued, Eleanor turned to a lady nearby and asked in a low voice, "Who is that gentleman?"

"That is Lord Merriot, my dear. I am sure we should all feel highly honored that he has condescended to come here at all. There are many I'm convinced who feel it would have been far better if he had stayed away."

"Good heavens, what has the poor man done?" asked Eleanor, considerably startled.

"Well, I was never one to repeat gossip," began her informant eagerly, "but they say he is most dreadfully loose with women, quite a libertine. They say he cannot lose at love or cards and that he's killed his man in a duel, too—more than one duel, mind!"

"*They* seem to say a great deal," Eleanor commented, regarding the gentleman with all the interest that such a condemnation inevitably aroused. "Surely he cannot be so *very* wicked?"

The lady shrugged. "I could not say, my dear, but I must own that he is an excessively attractive creature. For my part, I have never thought the worse of a man for being a rake."

Eleanor was shocked to find herself in sympathy with this view. Her interest was caught as it had not been in years. The gentleman's elegant, modishly-attired figure brought back to Eleanor memories of her youth when she had often danced with men of fashion, so different from the solid country squires she met in Pudsley. But as she studied his face she found herself drawn to the man himself. The look of reckless courage she read in his expression excited her. She half hoped that he would glance in her direction, but he showed little interest in the assembled ladies. Instead, accompanied by several other gentlemen, he made his way toward the card room.

Lord Merriot having left the room, Eleanor remembered she had duties to perform and looked about her for her errant niece. She saw her moving gracefully down the set with an unknown man. She was very sure he did not live in the neighborhood, yet there was something in his appearance that struck her as familiar. Impulsively, she turned to her informative neighbor and asked the name of Emily's partner.

"Why, my dear, that is Simon Trafford. Did you not catch his name? I must say it is quite a triumph for little Emily to have him to lead her out like this at her first appearance."

Eleanor turned pale. "Trafford? Isn't that the Lennox family name?"

"Why, yes, Eleanor. Simon Trafford is Viscount Lennox's son." The informant's eyes rested on Eleanor's face and were full of curiosity about the young woman's sudden agitation.

Quickly, Eleanor tried to pull herself together. "Goodness, it is hot in here, is it not?" she exclaimed, fanning herself vigorously. "So that is Lennox's son. I knew his mama and papa a little when I was in town."

As she spoke, she was aware that Mrs. Witherspoon was eyeing her speculatively. She could have screamed with vexation. Why had she allowed herself to show such emotion?

Had she betrayed herself? Suddenly she felt as though everyone was watching her and whispering. She longed to escape . . . and, perhaps might even have run from the room! But at that moment, Emily returned from the dance, smiling and happy. She was anxious to introduce Simon to her aunt for she thought him quite the most handsome, the most delightful young man she had yet encountered.

Eleanor fought the rising panic that threatened to engulf her as the young couple approached. She took a deep breath and held out a hand which, to her surprise, was quite steady.

"Mr. Trafford, I am so happy to meet you. Thank you for taking such good care of my niece." She spoke so calmly that Mrs. Witherspoon was obliged to own herself mistaken and agree that it must have been the heat that accounted for the paleness, as Eleanor had claimed.

"Why, ma'am, we have met before." Simon smiled, bowing over her hand. "Although I do not expect you to remember a scrubby schoolboy. We met at a picnic in Richmond park, and I thought you the most beautiful lady at the party. I was ten years old and fell madly in love with you!"

Miss Portland could not but respond to his charm, painful though the memory he conjured up was. "Indeed, now you put me in mind of it, I do remember. Emily, it seems as though your Mr. Trafford and I are old friends!"

Emily was not terribly interested in these reminiscences. She was concerned only with the question of whether her partner would ask her to stand up with him once more and if so whether or not she would be permitted to accept his offer.

She need not have worried. Simon duly begged permission to lead her onto the floor, and Eleanor graciously approved. They were by far the most attractive young couple, and she derived considerable pleasure from watching them. To be sure, it was a pity that they would be unable to pursue their acquaintance. Simon would no doubt return to London. For her own sake she was glad of it. The prospect of a connection between her own family and Lennox's was a nightmare. But surely it could do no harm to allow Emily to dance with a personable young man. Perhaps he would render her less easily pleased with the sort of young men who had led her off to see the moonlight at other parties.

By the time Emily once more joined her aunt, the Warrington party had arrived. Eleanor was invited to join them,

a prospect which gave her little pleasure. She disliked Sir
Charles intensely and pitied his gentle little wife. However, as
Lord Portland had been quite definite in his instructions, she
obligingly sat with Lady Warrington while Emily went off, not
altogether happily, upon the arm of Mr. George.

"May I say, Miss Portland, how pleased I am to see you
here?" began Lady Warrington in her soft voice. "Such a lovely
gown."

"Thank you, Lady Warrington. But please, will you call me
Eleanor? We have known each other long enough, I think."

"Indeed we have," responded the little lady. "My name is
Rosamund, if you should care to use it."

"How pretty!" exclaimed Eleanor. The two ladies settled
down to a comfortable talk, only to be interrupted by the sudden
appearance of Sir Charles. He frowned as he listened to their
conversation and heard his wife address Eleanor by her Christian name. Hardly troubling to lower his voice he admonished
his wife.

"It is necessary, ma'am, to recognize that woman if there
is to be a family connection, but I do not wish you to be upon
such familiar terms with her."

Poor Lady Warrington turned fiery red and stammered
something inaudible. Eleanor was furious, but out of charity
for her companion she decided to pretend she had heard nothing. She continued to chatter and if her gaiety was a little
forced, no one present knew her well enough to detect it.

All in all, it was a considerable relief to Miss Portland when
they were at last able to leave that eventful ball, and she could
sink once more back against the cushions of his lordship's
carriage. The evening had ended on a note of mortification,
yet she felt more alive than she had in years. Instead of hiding
from her detractors she had gone boldly out to face them and
had in consequence discovered that there was nothing so very
dreadful to be feared. Perhaps she should go about a little more
after all. People would become accustomed to seeing her again,
and she would grow more and more comfortable in company
too. At the back of her mind lay the hope that should she
emerge from her retirement, she just might encounter the dashing Lord Merriot.

As for Emily, snuggling in her dark corner, her thoughts
were all of Simon. She daydreamed they were in love and he
came to carry her off in the teeth of her father's cruel opposition,

possibly shooting that odious George Warrington in the process.

In the days that followed the delightful evening, Emily complained repeatedly about everything seeming sadly flat. Secretly, Eleanor agreed. But she was more fortunate because she had so much to do. Poor Emily only sat and thought of a suitor who did not appear.

Miss Portland had taken over most of her sister-in-law's duties. It must be said that the house was very much better run than it had ever been before. She was able to untangle even the most difficult domestic problem with a little tact, whereas Lady Portland had never considered it necessary to be tactful with servants.

Not only did Eleanor have the duties of her sister-in-law to perform, she had many of her own. For years she had devoted herself to the poor of the Parish. She did not play Lady Bountiful, distributing warm soup to a few children and exhorting them to attend church more regularly. Instead she entered their homes, listened to their problems, and suggested practical solutions. She was on friendly terms with the tenants, too, and visited them regularly, reporting to her brother which barn wanted rethatching and which fences needed mending. She was very popular with the villagers, and the fact they were quite well aware of her history made them even more appreciative of her. So the nobs ostracized her! Well, the poor would have more sense! They loved her.

A lady so interested in the Parish might have worked closely with the vicar. This was not the case with Eleanor, however, because she had scant respect for the Reverend Higginbottom. A pompous, ill-educated man. He cared far more for his dinner and glass of port than he did for the spiritual needs of his flock.

He was often unpleasantly familiar with Eleanor. She supposed he felt entitled to behave so toward a woman with a dubious past. He was careful to display the fullest respect for her when in the presence of Lord Portland, though, and as she scarcely ever met him alone, his manner did not worry her over-much.

Although it was still very early in the year, a few daffodils had been encouraged by the early sunshine to show themselves in the sheltered dales. Eleanor had plucked a quantity and carried them to the church to decorate the altar. This was something she had begun some years ago, and she derived a great deal of pleasure from the occupation.

It was dark in the little Norman church, and despite a huge wood-burning stove, freezingly cold. Eleanor finished her business as quickly as possible and was preparing to hurry out into the wintry sunshine when the doorway was blocked by the stout frame of the Reverend Higginbottom.

"Miss Portland, how very pleasant. I had hoped to find you here. I was sure you would not allow a little cold weather to keep you from your work of beautifying our little house of God."

"I fear my efforts today are sadly commonplace," answered Eleanor ruefully. "There is little to be done with a few daffodils in the way of artistic arrangement."

The vicar smiled condescendingly and shook his head. "You are far too modest, ma'am. Your sure touch brings splendor to our humble church."

Eleanor did not at all care for these fulsome compliments. Drawing on a pair of serviceable York tan gloves, she moved toward the door.

"Good day, Mr. Higginbottom," she said coolly, giving a civil nod to the reverend gentleman.

"Pray, ma'am, will you not allow me to accompany you to Hawthorne Place? The evening draws in, soon it will be quite dark. I could not rest easy should you venture alone," he told her, offering his arm.

Eleanor did not wish at all for this escort, but she knew of no polite way to refuse him. She placed her hand upon his arm and chatted amiably enough upon Parish matters as they strolled along the deserted lane.

Nothing occurred to alarm her until suddenly, without any warning, the vicar broke roughly in upon what she was saying about the matter of little Willy Proctor's broken leg.

"My dear, nay dearest, Miss Portland, you must hear me!" He seized her hand and spoke in a loud, impassioned burst. "It cannot be unknown to you that it has long been my dearest hope, my most fervent desire to beg you to be mine!"

Eleanor was considerably startled. "Mr. Higginbottom, I do not understand you, sir!"

The reverend gentleman abruptly dropped the theatrical tone he had used, his voice becoming unpleasantly warm and oily. "Oh, come now, my dear," he said, sliding his arm around her waist. "You know very well what is in my mind. Eleanor, you are the helpmate the Lord in his infinite wisdom has chosen for me. You are..."

"I do not think, sir, that I have given you permission to use my given name," interrupted Eleanor frostily. "Have the goodness to release me at once!"

He laughed. "That's what I like in you—the haughty air. But there is no need for it between us. I know very well why you have come so often to decorate the church, and why you have taken such an interest in the rag-and-tag of the Parish. Well, my dear, you have succeeded in capturing my attention. You are a damned fine woman!" With this he rather inexpertly attempted to plant a kiss upon her lips.

"How dare you?" demanded Eleanor, pale with fury. "How dare you touch me?"

"Do not play off those innocent missish airs," he told her angrily. "I know very well that I am not the first. I suppose my kisses are not good enough for you!"

Eleanor was shaking with rage and quite unable to answer him as she wished. Instead she said in a voice of icy politeness, "I would have you know, sir, that even had you made your offer to me in less impertinent terms and spared me these insults, I still would have refused to ally myself with one for whom I feel nothing but contempt!"

He turned a dull red and blustered, "Think well, ma'am. You may live to regret this decision. There are not many men as willing as I to take another man's leavings!"

"Oh," gasped Eleanor, bringing up her hand to deal him a stinging blow. He caught her hand, and before she knew what he was about, he had jerked her roughly into his arms. His thick, wet lips came down upon hers while his arms clamped her against his chest. Though a tall woman and a strong one, she was quite helpless against him. His hand began to wander feverishly over her body, and she felt sick with disgust at his touch.

Suddenly she heard a carriage rattling up the lane toward them. Her desperate hope was that a passenger would come to her aid, but instead the carriage went swaying by, sending a spray of muddy water over them both.

"Damn it! What was that?" The vicar lifted his head, slackened his hold.

Eleanor didn't stay to inform him. She whisked herself out

of his embrace and set off down the road without so much as a backward glance.

"Did you see that?" demanded one occupant of the carriage to the other.

"Indeed I did. Shameless, quite shameless. To embrace in such a fashion on the open road like that!"

"Of course, my dear, you saw who it was. Eleanor Portland. Well, it just goes to show how you can be deceived in people!"

"I for one was never deceived. Once loose, always loose, if you ask me. All those die-away airs of hers never took me in for a moment."

"Why, do you think she has been carrying on like this all these years?" demanded the lady excitedly.

"I should think it more than likely," answered the other with a malicious smile.

"But whoever with? There are not so many gentlemen in the neighborhood."

"Who knows, my dear?" The woman shrugged. "With *that* kind anyone will do. Even one of the grooms!"

Naturally neither of these good ladies wasted a moment in relaying the news of what they had seen. Though few people were credulous enough to believe all the ladies would have them believe about Eleanor, it was generally felt she had deceived them into accepting her back into their circle. With one accord they were resolute in banishing her once more.

The first indication of all this reached Miss Portland from one of the most formidable matrons of her acquaintance while walking in the village. Although she had not been used to being treated with anything more than common politeness by this lady, the cut puzzled her.

It was only the first of many such incidents. Several dinner parties to which she had been bidden with her brother were mysteriously canceled. Worst of all, Emily was no longer asked to parties. All in the county were fond of Emily, but they could not have her without inviting her aunt, and so they preferred to do without them both. Only Harriet remained faithful, and it was she who eventually summoned up the courage to explain the sudden turn of events to her idol.

Emily, who had suffered much in the past few days, was confiding her woes to her sympathetic friend.

"Harry, I simply do not understand it. I know for a fact that Cynthia Draycott intended to ask me to her party and now I find that it was held last night and I was never invited at all. What is the matter, Harriet? What have I done wrong?"

Harriet put her arm around her drooping friend. "Silly, you haven't done anything wrong. It has nothing to do with you at all!"

Emily sniffed. "Then there *is* something. I knew it! Tell me, Harriet, please tell me."

Her friend shook her head. "Do not ask, Emmy. I cannot tell you. It is too . . . too . . ."

"Tell us, Harriet," came a calm voice. Unobserved, Eleanor had entered the room. She sank gracefully into the chair opposite and studied the little face in front of her.

"Oh, Miss Portland, I cannot," averred the unhappy Harriet.

"You must, my dear. If it makes it any easier I may as well tell you that I have a pretty good idea what the problem is. I should like to know the whole, if you please."

Haltingly, Harriet related the gossip that was circulating around the village. "But I do not believe a word of it, Miss Portland, not one word of it!"

"Thank you, sweetheart. It appears you are alone in that. Strange, I had thought I had friends here. Obviously I was wrong."

All at once her calm deserted her. Hiding her lovely face in her hands she began to cry as though her heart would break. The two girls were horrified to see the elegant Eleanor so overset. They hovered around her, murmuring her name and planting timid kisses upon her hair. Such treatment quickly restored her. She wiped away her tears with a watery smile, saying, "It is not that I am hurt, my dears. It just makes me so dreadfully angry to be condemned unheard like this! Oh, I should like to throttle those hateful scandalmongers!"

The girls watched with some awe as she began to pace up and down the room, reminding Harriet of a wild lioness she had once been taken to see at a traveling fair.

Abruptly, she stopped and turned to Emily, her face alive with excitement. "Emily! Emily, do you still wish to go to London?" she demanded in a ringing voice.

Emily jumped up and threw herself into her aunt's arms. "Yes! Oh, yes, Aunt Eleanor!" she cried. "That will show them!"

"Yes, I rather think it will," declared Eleanor, in quite her old manner. "I will not spend the rest of my life trying to win the good opinion of these petty-minded country people. Damnation to the lot of them! We will go to London!"

chapter 3

Eleanor awoke with a start to find herself in unfamiliar surroundings. For a moment she could not imagine where she might be, but as sleep receded, she remembered and lay back upon her pillows with a sigh. It was the strident call of a street vendor that had awakened her and now the unaccustomed noise of early morning in a London street prevented her from drifting back into slumber. Instead she lay thinking about the events of the past month. A month of great importance in her life.

Lord Portland, when made aware of his sister's sudden change of heart, had been unable to conceal his relief. He allowed her no time to change her mind again but whisked his family along the post roads to London in time which would have done credit to His Majesty's Mail. Eleanor protested at this unseemly haste, declaring that they had not time even to prepare their wardrobes. Lord Portland, however, generously promised them as many clothes as they desired once they were in London, which silenced his sister most effectively. In truth, having made her decision, she was as anxious to be gone as he.

Her brother had acquired a handsome house in the most

modish part of town. The neat modern building in South Audley Street was just what Eleanor would have wished for. The situation was convenient for the Park and for the shops of Piccadilly and yet was still secluded from the worst bustle of the town.

Eleanor could not conceal from herself that she felt extremely nervous that first morning as she and Emily set forth to explore. She fancied she saw Lennox in every male figure that appeared, only to find as they came up with these gentlemen that they bore no resemblance to his lordship whatsoever. Gradually, she ceased to expect him and began to enjoy the outing, stimulated by the colorful sights and the noise. They returned in a gay mood to find that several people had called while they were gone and had left cards with them. Most of these visitors were unknown to Eleanor. However, picking up one particularly elegant gilt-edged card, she exclaimed, "Why, this is from Lady Jersey. How kind of her to call upon us! I remember her well. She was always very good to me, and I shall be so happy to meet her again!"

Emily was impressed. Even in Pudsley they had heard of the great Lady Jersey. "Goodness, Aunt, how thrilling! I do hope she will call again."

She called in fact the very next morning. She was a stylish, animated little lady given to odd humors but her affections, when fixed, were steadfast. She had been an intimate friend of Eleanor's late mama and had taken maternal interest in her first visit to London. Now she greeted her warmly, calling her a wicked creature for staying away from them all so long. She pinched Emily's chin and complemented her on her gown, but it was apparent that the purpose of her visit was to talk to Eleanor alone. Emily, although not usually quick to take a hint, was obliged to leave the two ladies alone together.

Lady Jersey leaned forward and took Eleanor's hands in hers. "My dear, she is a sweet pretty child, but I am glad she is gone for I wish to talk to you. Oh, I know I have not the smallest right to interfere but your mother was my dearest friend and I have always been so fond of you, Eleanor."

"I know it, ma'am, and I have always been most grateful for your affection," answered Eleanor warmly.

"Then you will not think me a horrid prying old woman if I ask you a rather delicate question. Tell me, my dear, have you quite forgotten Lennox?"

"Forgotten? No, ma'am. How could I forget? If you mean does the memory still pain me, I can only answer . . . sometimes."

"I have put myself badly, Eleanor," said Lady Jersey, gently pressing her young friend's hand. "Do you still love him?"

Eleanor flushed. "To be quite honest with you, Lady Jersey, I do not know. You see, I have lived such a retired life and met so few gentlemen that his image is as strong for me now as it was when I . . . Well, you understand me. But I am very well aware that the man I held so dear is now ten years older and may be a very different person, as I am. When I have seen him, I may be able to answer your question, but now I cannot."

Her visitor smiled. "I have no doubt you think me impertinent for asking such questions, but I do have a reason. You see, my love, the scandal is an old one, but it is not forgotten. For the moment, people are willing to wait and see how you conduct yourself. I am not quite a nobody you know and many will follow my lead. I shall procure you vouchers for Almacks; that, my dear, is the utmost I can do. However, I will give you a very good piece of advice if you care to hear it."

"Please do, ma'am," she answered with a slight smile.

"Very well, it is this—do not under any circumstances apologize for the past! Do not hang your head and beg forgiveness of the world or the world will inevitably turn its back on you. Show people you care nothing for their opinion, and they will fawn on you. Believe me, my dear, for I know what I am talking about."

"I do, ma'am, and I thank you. It is good advice, and I mean to take it," declared Eleanor with spirit.

Lady Jersey embraced her lightly. "You will do, my love. Now remember, I shall expect to see you at Almacks and let us have no faint hearts. Let me tell you that you are twice as beautiful now as you were all those years ago and very much more interesting!"

Eleanor laughed, but when the little lady had swept from the room she devoted a good deal of thought to what she had said. She remembered that the great Mr. Brummell himself had always held it as one of his maxims that one should never apologize and never admit a fault. It seemed to her that if such worldly personages as Lady Jersey and Mr. Brummell advised it, then it must in truth be the right way to go about things. Very well, the world should see!

In pursuance of these excellent plans, Eleanor visited all the

most modish mantua makers with Emily and the newly-arrived
Harriet in tow. Emily soon lost interest in the proceedings for
she was to be allowed to wear nothing but the most demure
of white muslins. It gave her little pleasure to watch her aunt
being fitted for precisely the sort of gown she dreamed of wearing
herself. Harriet, however, was entranced to see that her idol
appeared more elegant in each gown she purchased.

All these preparations had taken time. There was the hair-
dresser to be summoned, the bootmaker, and the glove maker
to visit. However, this was the day chosen by Eleanor to mark
their real entry into Society, for in the afternoon they would
drive in the Park. She had already chosen the gown she would
wear: apple-green crepe with a dark green velvet spencer and
a saucy quilted bonnet trimmed with swansdown. Emily, as
befitted a debutante, would appear in pale primrose muslin,
while Harriet had decided on a gown of fawn cambric trimmed
with cherry ribbons. Emily instantly perceived it was far more
distinguished than her own pretty gown.

Eleanor thought that together they presented a picture to
take even the jaded *ton* by surprise.

She stretched luxuriously and rang the bell. The abigail who
brought her morning chocolate had conceived a passionate admiration for Eleanor and so, having laid the tray upon her lap,
drawn the curtains and stoked the fire, she lingered in the hope
of a chat with her mistress.

"Thank you, Lucy," said Miss Portland with a smile. "The
chocolate is just as I like it."

"Well, miss, I make sure they do it right in the kitchen and
I don't let them put too much sugar in 'cause I know you don't
like it."

"That is good of you, Lucy," said Eleanor pleasantly. "Tell
me, is it sunny outside?"

"Yes, miss, it's lovely. Not too cold and ever so bright.
There'll be crocuses out in the Park likely," answered Lucy
eagerly.

Eleanor pushed back the covers and swung her shapely legs
over the side of the bed. "Well, I must get up. I am getting
so lazy, lying in bed until half the morning is over. Oh, Lucy,
it is so nice to be able to do just as I like again!"

Lucy did not quite understand her mistress's remark, for
she had always assumed that the Quality did just as they chose

upon every occasion, but she bobbed a curtsey and smiled, pleased to see her mistress in such spirits.

It was exciting to be appearing before the *ton* for the first time. Although to the uninitiated the prospect of a sedate drive in Hyde Park might seem less than wonderful, Eleanor was well aware that everyone who was anyone in Society might be seen promenading there between the hours of three and five.

It appeared that most of the Polite World had assembled by the time their carriage rattled smartly along the circular road already teeming with fashionable vehicles. They attracted no little attention, firstly because the sight of three unknown and modishly dressed young women naturally aroused the interest of the *ton* and secondly as some of the older generation recognized Eleanor and hurried to impart the news of her reappearance to their fellows.

On the whole, the company was pleased to see her once more. They were willing to forgive a great deal in a woman as beautiful and well dressed as she. However, the scandal was not by any means forgotten, and there were many who reserved judgment. The important thing was that Eleanor did not have to suffer the mortification of being cut by her former acquaintances and instead received stately bows from a number of ladies who might have been expected to condemn her. She did not know it but she had Lady Jersey to thank for this. She had visited all of her many acquaintances and reminded a great many of them of favors past not yet repaid. It was only necessary to hint to some noble dame with marriageable daughters that vouchers for Almacks might be withheld and their cooperation was assured.

Lady Jersey was not seen that afternoon, but several of the other haughty patronesses of Almacks were there. Mrs. Drummond Burrell contented herself with only a distant bow, but kind Lady Sefton ordered her coachman to pull alongside the Portland ladies and was most solicitous as to their welfare.

"So delightful to have you returned to us, Miss Portland. I do hope you have settled in comfortably."

"Thank you, Lady Sefton, we have a very neat little house in South Audley Street. I could not wish for more pleasant lodgings," answered Eleanor.

"Why, how fortunate. You are quite near me for I am in Curzon Street, you know. That gives me such an idea! I am giving a small reception tonight. Nothing at all elaborate, just a few friends. I know it is very short notice but if you are not engaged for this evening, would you care to come? The young ladies too, of course, although there is to be no dancing and you will be sadly bored, you poor children. It would be a good way for you all to make some new acquaintances, would it not?"

Eleanor was not so ignorant as to be unaware of the very great honor being paid her. Lady Sefton's little soirées were famous for the qualities of wit and brilliance in the people who congregated in her spacious rooms. Many of the *ton* angled in vain for such an invitation for years. Lady Sefton had clearly taken them under her wing.

Eleanor blushed and answered with real gratitude. "Ma'am, I cannot thank you sufficiently for your kindness. We would love to come to your party, would we not, girls?"

Emily and Harriet, who were quite tired of sitting in night after night, nodded vigorously. "Yes, indeed," they chorused.

The ladies chatted for a few minutes longer until it was borne upon Lady Sefton that she was blocking the way of a rakish gentleman in a sporting curricle. She glanced over her shoulder and threw a careless greeting to this gentleman and then passed on allowing the curricle to come alongside the barouche. The driver of the vehicle glanced at the ladies in the barouche and it was apparent that he found a great deal to admire for his gaze lingered until Eleanor lifted her eyes to meet his. She found herself gazing into cool gray eyes and dropped her own quickly, feeling the rosy color stealing into her cheeks. She recognized him at once—Lord Merriot. Her heart seemed almost to miss a beat as his eyes held hers. It had been a long time since any man had looked at her in quite that way. The strength of her response to him frightened her. Fortunately, the carriages were separated by the movement of the traffic and she saw no more of him.

It was growing late and Eleanor had just decided that it was time they returned to the house when Emily suddenly exclaimed, "Look! Oh, Aunt Eleanor, look over there! Isn't that Mr. Trafford?" She waved her hand, almost bouncing in her seat with excitement. "Oh, he has seen us. He is coming this way! Harriet, what shall I say? How do I look? Is my bonnet straight? Did I not tell you he was handsome?"

She chattered nervously on, unaware of the sudden pallor

upon her aunt's lovely face. Eleanor sat rigidly staring directly in front of her so that her profile was hidden from the approaching gentlemen.

Simon hurried to the carriage. He was delighted to see Emily once more for she had been much in his thoughts and it had gone to his heart to leave her as he had without seeing her again. He questioned her eagerly about her situation. Might he visit her? Where did she reside? Should he see her at Almacks? She answered him gaily, her always pretty face so lit from within that she looked beautiful.

Eleanor heard Simon beg Emily's permission to present his companion to her and then, remembering his manners he said, "Miss Portland, may I present my father, Viscount Lennox?"

She turned her head and for the first time in ten years met the incredulous eyes of her lover.

She nodded but was quite unable to answer his polite inquiry as to her health. The power of speech seemed to have deserted her. Nor was Lennox in a much better state. His manner was constrained and embarrassed, he seemed content to let his son talk, answering in a preoccupied tone any remarks addressed to him. Each was intent upon their own emotions and would have been hard put to describe exactly what these were. Eleanor felt strangely detached and cold. It occurred to her that despite all her good resolutions she had really come to London in the hope of rekindling their love but now he was before her, she felt little but an aching sense of loss.

The Viscount's feelings were of an equally complex nature. His desire for her which had always mastered him had surged forward as though the ten years of separation had never been and yet he found himself hoping that she would go away as suddenly as she had reappeared. He did not wish his comfortable life to be disrupted once more. He had settled down into an amicable arrangement with Alyce in which she went her own way and he mounted a series of very expensive mistresses. Life was pleasant these days and he was really far too old for romance. Yet as he studied her lovely face, the memory of their one night together could not but return. None of his mistresses, expert though they were, could recapture for him the brief ecstasy he had known with her.

Suddenly she lifted her downcast eyes and met his in one long look. It seemed to him she was searching for something in his face. She was, but she did not find it. He was nothing more to her than a pleasant stranger, this man whom she had loved, who had seduced her and left her to spend the rest of her life in disgrace and seclusion.

She sighed and then in a voice of surprising calm she said, "So glad to have met you again, Mr. Trafford, but I think we must be getting back now. Good day, Lord Lennox."

The barouche started forward leaving the two gentlemen standing by the side of the road, staring after them.

It was to be expected that this encounter should have caused Eleanor considerable distress. She was able to hide her emotions from the girls for both were far too taken up with rhapsodizing upon the many perfections of the son to notice anything odd in Miss Portland's reaction to the father. Indeed, they had barely noticed the older man and had they done so they would hardly have associated him with Eleanor's dashing and mysterious lover. The rakish gentleman who had so stared them out of countenance was very much more the image of a noble seducer.

Preoccupied though she was, Eleanor could not fail to perceive that Emily was already in a fair way to fancying herself in love and it worried her for both their sakes. Simon was of course a charming young man but she did not think that the Viscount would regard a marriage between the two any more favorably than she did herself. Probably he would look a good deal higher for a wife for his heir.

She tried to hint this in a few words to her niece but Emily was not to be dampened. Although they had hardly exchanged one intimate word, she was as sure of Simon's feelings as she was of her own and so her aunt's cautious words were quite wasted.

They parted as soon as they entered the house for the two girls wished to be alone to talk secrets and Eleanor longed for the sanctuary of her own bedchamber. Once there she threw herself down upon the bed and indulged in the luxury of a good cry which made her feel very much better. After all, she told herself, it was really as well to have got the meeting over so early and to have found herself quite indifferent rather than to have embarked once more upon a love affair that could hold out no greater hopes of happiness now than it had ten years earlier. She sat up and wiped her eyes with a defiant sniff. The past was past, she had laid her ghost and was ready to begin her life again.

• • •

It seemed important that she should look her very best that
night and she chose to wear a gown of spangled satin that so
caught the light she seemed to shimmer as she moved. Her hair
was dressed high upon the top of her head and allowed to fall
in becomingly careless ringlets about her ears. She draped a
light gauze scarf across her shoulders and around her neck she
clasped the pearls her mama had left her. When she had finished
she turned to the admiring Lucy and smiled. "Well, Lucy, what
do you think?"

"Oh, miss! You look a picture, a real picture. I don't believe
there's a lady in town as can touch you!" cried the servant
fervently.

Such praise was very welcome although it only confirmed
what her mirror had already told her. Eleanor went down with
her head held high and an odd feeling in her heart that tonight
was going to be very special for her.

Lady Sefton's little party was by far the most modish gath-
ering that Emily had ever attended and in consequence she
behaved very prettily, being far too shy to allow her high spirits
to lead her into unbecoming behavior. She and Harriet were
pronounced very sweet children by the ladies and as it was
known that Emily was her papa's only child, those matrons
with marriageable sons were particularly attentive.

Occasionally, Eleanor would have the sensation that she
was being watched and lifting her head she would catch some
lady regarding her or perhaps see two women with their heads
together talking animatedly. She had no doubt that she was the
subject of their discourse but she did not writhe under this
knowledge as once she would have done. She was able to shrug
and dismiss it from her mind, leaving the ladies to enjoy their
malicious gossip.

She was much sought after for her hostess had made it clear
that she was a favorite. In any event the gentlemen needed no
encouragement to talk to quite the loveliest lady in the room.
Eleanor was enjoying her evening so much that she did not
realize how late it had become until she heard Lady
Sefton exclaim in mock disapproval, "Good evening, my lord
Merriot. What a wicked creature you are to come to my party
just as it is finishing. I warn you, there is nothing left to eat
at all!"

A singularly attractive voice answered in a caressing tone.
"But my dear lady, how could you think that I came here to

eat? I crave only the refreshment of your presence."

Eleanor turned her head in time to see Lord Merriot bowing with grace over his hostess's hand. Lady Sefton laughed and rapped his knuckles with her fan. "Flatterer! I should be foolish indeed if I were to believe that."

He made some laughing rejoinder, but Eleanor noted that the laughter did not reach his eyes which remained cold and mocking. Nevertheless, his smile was attractive enough to cause many little feminine flutters about the room and more than one young lady, attracted by the slight air of danger about him, cast languishing looks in his direction.

Observing the scene, Eleanor felt a little annoyed with herself for falling so easily a victim to the man's attraction. She determined to be gone at once for it was already one o'clock and the carriage had been called for twelve. It was unforgivable to keep the coachman sitting upon the box in this freezing weather and she was still more angry with herself for being so inconsiderate. Unfortunately, although she could see Harriet chatting happily with another debutante, Emily was nowhere to be seen. Her loving aunt fervently hoped that she had not gone off with a young gentleman to inspect the conservatory or anything of that nature. She really did not feel in the mood to cope with such an escapade.

"Excuse me, ma'am. I believe that you have dropped your fan," came a soft voice just behind her and turning quickly she found herself staring into Lord Merriot's eyes which held an expression that left her feeling breathless and insufficiently clad.

"I . . . I . . . think that you are mistaken, sir," she stammered in confusion. "As you can see, I have my fan here."

He smiled. "True, but you see, I have at least opened the conversation. Our kind hostess is far too conscientious to introduce so beautiful a lady to a man of my reputation. That is no reason why I may not present myself, I hope. I am Merriot and you are Miss Portland, are you not?"

She returned his smile, appreciating his methods. "Do you think that Lady Sefton would disapprove of our talking together, then, sir? Perhaps I ought to take her advice."

"Undoubtedly, but I beg that you will not. You must know that there is no other lady in the room to touch you. You are causing quite a sensation tonight, I assure you."

Eleanor flushed. There was something in his tone that convinced her he knew her history and why she was the object of so much interest to the other guests. It distressed her to think that this man should have heard the gossip and perhaps have judged her to be a light woman. She did not stop to wonder why his opinion should be important to her but instead abruptly wished him good night and, catching sight of her errant charges, bustled them all out of the salon and into their carriage.

The next day, to her aunt's considerable surprise, Emily was out of bed and dressed long before her usual hour. She had insisted upon donning one of her prettiest gowns and had been tiresomely fidgety all the morning.

At about eleven o'clock, when Mr. Trafford was ushered into the room by the butler, who wore a distinct air of congratulation, Eleanor understood her niece's unusual behavior.

Simon entered with the air of one sure of his welcome. Nor was he disappointed. Emily was unaffectedly delighted to see him. She held out her hand to him and he caught it in his, holding it far longer than politeness warranted. Eleanor thought that he might just as well have kissed the chit and have done with it. Emily blushed a fiery red and could scarcely lift her eyes to meet his ardent gaze.

Very correctly Eleanor remained in the apartment with them although she was well aware that they both wished her at Jericho. She wondered with some irony whether her own experiences had made her a stricter chaperone. No doubt the usual doting maiden aunt would have slipped from the room to allow romance to take its course. But she knew, none better, the value of reputation and she intended to guard Emily's.

She sat quietly sewing and very soon the young people forgot that she was present at all. She could not but be amused as she listened to their discourse.

". . . he's the best hack I've ever put my leg over. A beautiful stepper with the softest mouth imaginable. I think him remarkably handsome too, four white socks, you may imagine how elegant. Of course, I ride very light but he could carry a far heavier man with ease, I assure you."

Eleanor laughed a little to see how fascinated Emily appeared by all this although if she knew one end of a horse from the other, it was as much as her aunt bargained for. Eleanor, on her part, was thankful that she was past the age of letting a man bore her to death while worshiping, figuratively, at his feet. Emily seemed to find nothing lacking in his discourse, however.

Harriet, who had been out of the house all morning paying a call upon an elderly relative, entered in time to hear Simon beg to be allowed to escort the ladies to a balloon ascension to be held in Hyde Park the following afternoon. Emily was naturally all agog to go and Eleanor could see that Harriet was equally inclined to accept the treat. With a shrug, she resigned herself and gave her consent.

"Certainly, Mr. Trafford. I am sure we would all enjoy the outing immensely." She was obliged to call her niece to order for hugging her violently. "If you would call for us at two we shall be ready to accompany you," she told him, patting into place the curls disarrayed by Emily's rapture.

"I wonder if I might bring my friend Montgomery along, ma'am. He is a splendid fellow and I know he would very much like to come with us," asked Simon tentatively.

"I see no reason why not," answered Eleanor, perceiving that she would be called upon to play gooseberry to two young couples who would no doubt pay not the slightest attention to her. Oh, well, that, after all, was what she had come to London to do.

Fortunately for the success of the expedition, the afternoon was bright and sunny. The ladies were tempted to venture forth in their prettiest bonnets and were delighted to learn that Simon intended to convey them to the Park in the smartest open barouche drawn by a matched pair of grays. Lord Montgomery was to ride alongside the carriage, but dismounted in order to be introduced.

"Most happy, ma'am," said this young gentleman with a bow of exquisite polish.

He appeared to be a gentleman of few words but his slightly protuberant eyes had brightened perceptibly at the sight of Harriet in a gown of pink taffeta. Eleanor was encouraged to hope that her little admirer might be able to form an even more eligible connection than Emily and she would be very happy to see her so fortunately situated. This was quite the only source of satisfaction she found in that entire afternoon of unrelieved boredom.

She was quite unable to feel any excitement as the huge balloon began to fill and when at last it was ready and instead of rising above the ground fell to earth with a crash, she felt that she might have expected it. Fortunately, no one was hurt but everyone agreed that the whole thing had been rather an anticlimax. Everyone except Simon and Emily, that is. They had been getting on famously and had already arrived at a degree of understanding which would have astounded her aunt.

"I suppose we had best wait a little while before I approach your father," Simon had said under cover of the excitement caused by the balloon's downfall.

"Oh, yes. They would never believe that we could know our minds so quickly. One cannot explain that we fell in love all in a moment, they would not understand," said Emily, convinced that no adult could ever have been in love as she and Simon were.

"Was it so with you, too? I could not stop thinking of you all this time and then when I saw you again . . . Dearest little Emily. To think that you felt the same way and if you had not come to town I should never have known it. Do you think that your father will have any objection?"

Dearly as Emily would have liked to picture herself as a persecuted heroine she was obliged to own that her father would in all probability be delighted to learn of her engagement. Nor did Simon anticipate any difficulty, yet he was loath to approach his own father. He had noticed some slight reserve on Lennox's part when they had encountered the ladies in the Park. It did not occur to him that the Viscount had hardly noticed his Emily.

"I think we should wait for about a month or so, my sweet," he told her. "There can be no accusation then of haste. After all, what possible objection can anyone have to our marriage? There can be nothing to stop us, Emily, nothing at all."

chapter 4

Although Emily considered herself to be a damsel of more than ordinary sophistication, she was by no means too old to enjoy an outing to some of the less modish haunts that London had to offer. Eleanor, who retained delightful memories of a visit to Astley's famous Amphitheatre, conducted her charges to this and several other inelegant entertainments. Lord Portland was far too busy at his club—where his devoted sister suspected he did little other than sleep away the hours before dinner—to be of any use to Eleanor in these jaunts. Simon and Lord Montgomery, however, were only too eager to be escorts.

Eleanor, watching the growing intimacy between her niece and Mr. Trafford with some disapprobation, attempted discreetly to discover how far things had gone, but she could get nothing from Emily beyond airy assurances.

"Do not concern yourself, dearest Aunt. Mr. Trafford is most amusing and obliging. That is all," she declared untruthfully in reply to Eleanor's delicate questioning.

"My dear Emily, I hope you understand that you are really far too young to make your choice now. Also, there are reasons that I cannot go into that make me fear for your happiness. I

43

do not think that this match would meet with your papa's approval. Nor the Viscount's for that matter."

Emily pouted. "Well, I think it is a little unfair that you should expect me to give up Simon's ... I mean Mr. Trafford's friendship, without even telling me the reason," she complained.

"You misunderstand me, Emily. I only meant to warn you against becoming too fond of Simon. He is a dear boy but believe me, it would not do at all."

"Well, it does not matter, for there are several other gentlemen that I like just as well," Emily declared mendaciously.

"I am glad of that." Eleanor smiled, satisfied for the moment. "Now where would you like to go today. Shall it be the Tower or the Royal Exchange?"

"If you would like to know where I should really like to go, I will tell you," said Emily with a naughty look.

"Where?" demanded her aunt with foreboding.

"Saint Bartholemew's Fair at Smithfield," she answered demurely.

"Emily! You know that it is out of the question. You will meet no one there but a lot of ... It is not a place for respectable people," said her aunt firmly.

"Oh, but if Simon and Frederick were to accompany us there could be no objection. They have a bearded lady they say and the tallest man in the world. A play is performed called *Phantom of the Castle*. Oh, it would be such fun!"

Eleanor found it easy to withstand this list of attractions. "I am sorry, my dear, but no. Let us go to the Tower instead. They have a very fine collection of wild beasts, I believe, and there is a lovely view of the city from Tower Hill."

"Who wants to look at a moldy old city when one could be looking at the bearded lady," grumbled Emily. Nevertheless, she ran upstairs to change her gown, for Simon was to call for them at eleven and it was already past ten o'clock.

Harriet presently appeared, very elegant in a pelisse of Hussar green, daringly embellished with military epaulets of gold braid. She seemed happy and excited. Eleanor assumed that Lord Montgomery had continued with his attentions. Personally she found him a very dull young man but no doubt it was his dumb adoration that appealed to Harriet who had never before enjoyed the novel experience of being worshiped. Under the influence of his admiration she had unfurled new and pretty petals.

"Good morning, Harriet. How lovely you look!" exclaimed Eleanor as she took in the full glories, not only of the pelisse, but of the smart military bonnet to be worn with it. "We are quite overshadowed, my dear!"

"You do not think it a little too daring?" asked Harriet, anxiously gazing at herself in the mirror.

"Not at all. Most becoming. It is quite in the mode and shows a very proper support for our brave soldiers in Spain."

"Oh, I had not thought of that!" exclaimed Harriet. "Yes, of course it does. I shall be proud to wear it."

Having settled this knotty problem, Eleanor had only to await the arrival of their escorts. She had grown quite used to shepherding the young people around the town, and as they all had very good manners she was never allowed to feel that they could have very well done without her presence. Today, however, she felt particularly alone. She could not help wishing, rather wistfully, that she too had some unexceptional gentleman to squire her about.

In common with most young people who spent a great deal of time in the metropolis, neither Mr. Trafford nor Lord Montgomery had visited the Tower before. They were roused to real interest by the various exhibits, and although a moving history of the many unfortunates who had perished upon the block was supplied by the well-read Harriet, they were a very merry little party.

Having thoroughly inspected the buildings, they began to stroll around the gardens. Eleanor, who was feeling a little wearied by so much gay chatter, stopped upon a little hill overlooking the river where there was a seat. She told the rest of them to go on and for a few peaceful minutes she allowed herself the indulgence of a little private reflection.

She found her thoughts turning, as they rather often did, to the wicked Lord Merriot. Surely he could not be so bad as gossip suggested. A lady such as Maria Sefton would have shunned the man if only half the rumors that circulated about him were true. Or was she one of his conquests? She half wished that she had not allowed her confusion to overcome her that night. He had seemed anxious to talk to her and she owned to herself that she would have been more than happy to gratify him. Did he perhaps admire her? It was an exciting possibility.

She could not deny that she had found him most attractive. His air of caring little what the world thought could not but appeal to one who had suffered so much from its censure. She liked too the strength that she read in his face and the rather sardonic humor in his eyes. Then she became aware that she was allowing her thoughts to dwell on dreams which, though pleasant, were totally without foundation. She dismissed them firmly and looked about her.

She saw Harriet, her hand upon Montgomery's arm, and called to her.

"Harriet, where is Emily? I thought that you were all together. Do not tell me they have gone wandering off together!"

"We were together, but they left us about quarter of an hour ago. Emily said that you knew all about it, Miss Portland. They are gone to Smithfield. To the Fair, you know. I am so sorry, I thought that it was all right...I thought that you knew!" exclaimed Harriet, noting the distress upon Eleanor's face.

"No, oh no! What am I to do? How long did you say that they had been gone?"

"Only about a quarter of an hour, ma'am," answered Lord Montgomery. "Had I better go after them?"

"Yes...'no...I do not know. I should not think that you would be able to persuade them to return with you, my lord. It would be better if I go. But what am I to do with you, Harriet? I cannot take you to that place. Frederick, you must escort Miss Milton home if you please."

Harriet cried out at this, saying that Miss Portland would have far greater need of Montgomery's escort than she would. "I can easily go home in a hackney carriage, Miss Portland," she assured her duenna.

"Certainly not, Harriet. Your father entrusted you to my care and he would be justifiably angry if he knew that I had allowed you to jaunt about town in a hackney. I shall be perfectly safe on my own, I am sure."

At that moment a gentlemanly-looking man who had been watching them for some time approached, somewhat diffidently.

"Forgive my intrusion, ma'am, but I could not help overhearing something of your problem. May I be of any assistance?"

She turned in surprise to find that she was being addressed by a gentleman of some fifty years, well dressed and with an indefinable air of authority. He was smiling pleasantly and seemed genuinely desirous of helping her. A rather dirty schoolboy stood a little way off, palpably disgruntled by his mentor's sudden interest in the other party.

"I say, it is Mr. Osborne, ain't it?" suddenly demanded Lord Montgomery.

"Why, Frederick, I have not seen you since you came down from Oxford. How is your father? Well, I trust? And your mama?"

"Both very well, thank you, sir. Miss Portland, allow me to present Mr. Osborne to you. An old friend of my father's. If you wouldn't mind giving Miss Portland your escort, sir, I daresay you will be able to find them easily enough. Emily kept on and on about some freak she wanted to see. A bearded lady, though why she should be so anxious to see that is certainly beyond my understanding. But that's where they'll be, not a doubt of it!"

Eleanor did not know what to say. She could not but regard Mr. Osborne's arrival on the scene as providential but she was doubtful of the propriety of accepting his offer. "You are more than kind, sir, but I believe I should not impose upon your good nature. No doubt you are here to show this young gentleman around the Tower. It would be a shame to cut short his treat."

"As to that, ma'am, we have already seen the greater part of the buildings. Timothy will not object to returning home. Will you, my boy?"

Thus reminded of his manners, Master Timothy made a very creditable bow and muttered something that could, if the company wished, be taken as an assent.

"Frederick, I know that you will see that he gets home safely," said Mr. Osborne.

"Oh, Father, I can easily go back by myself, I am not a child," protested Timothy, revolted by the suggestion that he needed to be taken home like a regular noddy.

"Nevertheless, you will do as you are told, my boy," replied his father in a tone that brooked no argument. "Now, ma'am. As I understand it, you wish to go to Smithfield as quickly as possible, so shall we be gone? I have my carriage at the gate."

There seemed nothing else to be done. "I am really extremely grateful to you, sir," she said as he handed her into the carriage.

"Have you been in town long?" he inquired politely as they bowled along.

"Only a few weeks, sir. Emily, the child who is missing, is to be presented this Season. Her mama was most unfortunately taken ill and so I agreed to come to act as chaperone."

"But surely you should be enjoying the Season yourself. Forgive me, but you cannot be very much older than your Emily yourself."

"Oh, I am, sir, I assure you. I have had my Season, a long time ago!"

He found it hard to believe that so beautiful a creature could have been in London before and remained unwed, but as her ring finger was quite bare, it was obviously so. She seemed unwilling to discuss the matter so he let it rest.

Smithfield was reached quickly, but when they arrived Eleanor gazed in despair at the sea of merrymakers gathered there. The Fair was justly popular and it seemed to Eleanor that half of London had taken a holiday to attend it.

"Mr. Osborne, I am afraid it is hopeless," she said, turning to her companion. "What should I do?"

"I think that our first step is to find this bearded woman we have heard so much about. Let us hope that the sight is fascinating enough to keep Miss Emily interested until we can get there. Allow me to help you down." He threw a few orders over his shoulder to the groom and offered Eleanor his arm. Osborne, a tall man, was able to see over the heads of most of the crowd and could read the signs luring the unwary into the various tents and stalls.

"Ah!" he declared, "there, if I mistake not, is the bearded lady. And there also I think are our truants. Tell me, is Emily a taking little thing with big brown eyes and dark ringlets?"

"Yes, she is indeed. Have you truly seen her? Is Simon with her?"

"If Simon is a devilish handsome young fellow with fair hair, yes he is," replied her companion. "I must say they seem to be having such a good time that it seems almost a pity to disturb them."

"I daresay they are but it was very naughty of Emily to run off like this. What is more, I am sure she told Simon that I had given them my permission. She was always a most untruthful little girl. She has been far too much indulged."

Mr. Osborne, while deprecating this severity, could not but agree for he was a father himself.

"Emily!" exclaimed Eleanor as they came up with the young couple. "Emily, you ought to be ashamed of yourself!"

"Oh, Aunt Eleanor, how you startled me!" cried Emily. "I did not think . . . that is, I did not expect . . ."

"I know you did not, Emily, and that is what I complain of. You never do think of the trouble and inconvenience that you cause. Did you really think that I could just go home and leave you out here with no one to look after you but Simon? What if you had been seen?"

"Oh, no one could possibly have seen us here," answered Emily confidently. "It is such fun, you have no idea! Why, we have already seen the most wonderful mermaid with a fish's tail and everything."

Simon, who had been looking extremely uncomfortable, interrupted this flow. "I hope you don't think that I would have brought Emily here if I had known that you disapproved, ma'am. I would not have had this happen for the world, I assure you!"

"I daresay, you would not, Simon, but what made you think that I had given my permission for such an outrageous scheme?"

He looked even more unhappy, but was spared the necessity of answering by Emily who airily admitted that she had told him so. "For I knew that he would not bring me here otherwise."

"So you lied to Simon as well as scheming to deceive me?" said Eleanor coolly.

Emily's face crumpled and her eyes filled with tears. "It was not a lie . . . I was just . . ."

Eleanor's heart, as always, melted at the sight of her niece in tears. She placed her arm around the sobbing child and hugged her tightly. "My dear, I know that this was just a prank, but what I am trying to point out to you is that you can no longer indulge in such actions and expect everyone to laugh as they used to when you were a little girl. You are a young lady now. Come, do not cry anymore, for I know that you did not mean any harm."

"Oh, I am sorry! I did not think of it like that. I should not have told Simon a fib. Simon, I am so sorry. Please forgive me."

Mr. Trafford would have given much to have exchanged places with Miss Portland and to have put his own arms around his unhappy Emily. "My dear, there is nothing to forgive," he murmured.

Eleanor glanced quickly at him, taken aback by the note of unmistakable tenderness in his voice. Had matters progressed so far already?

She patted Emily upon the shoulder and spoke in bracing terms. "Well, since we are here and Mr. Osborne has kindly lent us his countenance, I do not see why we should not have a look at some of the sights. I must say that I would very much like to have a look at this mermaid of yours. And the two-headed dwarf. What do you say, sir? Can you spare us a little more of your time?"

He laughed and offered his arm. "I should be delighted, ma'am, for to tell you the truth I have not been so diverted in years. Lead on, young Trafford, to the two-headed dwarf!"

So the day ended more successfully than could reasonably have been expected. Mr. Osborne proved to be an entertaining companion, far more approachable than he had at first appeared. He and Eleanor were soon on the best of terms.

They returned to South Audley Street in time for tea. Both ladies had agreed that it would be far kinder not to tell Harriet what an exciting time she had missed.

Mr. Osborne, meanwhile, had returned home very thoughtful. There was, he was convinced, some mystery connected with the beautiful Miss Portland. He was quite determined to know more of her. He had never, since his much loved wife had died, cared for feminine companionship, but an afternoon in Eleanor's company had reminded him of how greatly an intelligent and lovely woman could enhance a man's life.

After a lonely dinner, he set out for his club where he was hailed by several men as he entered. Seeing a group of old friends gathered by the fireplace, he strolled across the room to greet them.

"Hey there, Osborne!" called Mr. Crowther, an old crony of his. "Now, who was that stunner I saw you driving this afternoon, you dog? Damn my eyes if I ever saw a lovelier creature. I warn you, I'll do my best to cut you out!"

"I fancy that you must be referring to Miss Eleanor Portland," answered Osborne, striving to appear unconcerned.

"What, not old Portland's daughter?" demanded the other in amazement.

"I believe so. Why?"

Mr. Crowther shrugged. "Well, it's up to you of course, old fellow, but I would not have thought that a woman of her kind was quite your type."

"I do not understand you, sir. What kind of woman?"

"Don't you know, then?" said Crowther, delighted to have the opportunity of enlightening his friend.

"Know what?" demanded Osborne.

"Why, the scandal, of course. I'm surprised you don't remember it. Caused a devilish stir at the time. That's the girl who ran off with Lennox, years ago. You can't have forgotten about it."

"Good God, man, are you sure? The Miss Portland I met is a lady!"

"No one ever said that she wasn't, old fellow. Fact remains. Damaged goods, my boy, damaged goods. Wouldn't touch it if I were you."

"You will apologize for that remark, Crowther," said Osborne angrily. "How dare you bandy a lady's name around the club in that manner?"

"No offense, no offense. I had no idea that you... Well, if that's the way it is, I'm sorry I said what I did. I'm sure she is as virtuous as you please these days. I daresay, no one will bother to rake up all that old dirt. But I beg you will not feel that you have to defend the lady's reputation against everyone who makes a simple remark or you'll be remarkably busy!"

Mr. Crowther spoke more truly than he knew. Even the patronage of such leaders of the fashionable world as Lady Jersey and Lady Sefton could not wholly protect Eleanor against malicious tongues. Perhaps had they been less ready to make much of her, other ladies would have been kinder. But for those women who had for years been attempting to enter the charmed circles into which Eleanor had so easily been drawn, there was no greater delight than in spreading and embellishing the story.

If Eleanor was aware of these sentiments, she gave no sign. She strictly adhered to Lady Jersey's advice and appeared everywhere, seemingly quite unconscious that she was the subject of impertinent gossip. The scandalmongers, frustrated by this indifference, became all the more virulent. Society could not make up its mind whether to accept Eleanor or not.

Lady Sefton was worried by this state of affairs and called upon her dear friend Sally Jersey to discuss the matter.

She found Lady Jersey still *deshabillée*, sipping rich chocolate and in a desultory way pursuing her morning mail. Lady
Jersey on her part was delighted to see Lady Sefton but dis-
inclined to take a serious view of the situation.

"My dear Maria, you are making too much of this. What
does it matter what a parcel of nobodies think?"

"That is all very well for you, Sally, with your position in
the world, but it is not so for Eleanor. Gossip can still hurt
her. You know how fond I am of her but really I must say that
she does not go out of her way to conciliate people. She should
bend a little more," was Lady Sefton's opinion.

"Not at all, my love. Eleanor is behaving precisely as I
advised her. She must force them to accept her, not beg them.
They will tear her to pieces if she weakens. They are just
waiting for the chance!"

"How I wish that she could meet some eligible gentleman.
It is ridiculous that such a lovely creature should be playing
nursemaid to a pair of silly children!"

"I could not agree more, my love, and if you can conjure
up a suitable parti, I for one would be very grateful. Do you
know I have hardly enjoyed the Season at all for I have been
too concerned about Eleanor to have a moment's peace."

Lady Sefton, who had observed her friend the previous
evening in scintillating form and enjoying herself hugely, made
a noncommittal reply to this and was soon lost in thought.

"Well, there is . . . No, he will not do," she began. "Perhaps
Fortesque? No, he is a little young for Eleanor. What do you
think of Barclay?"

"Very little," answered her ladyship succinctly.

"You are right, he has taken to drinking heavily lately. Do
you think that Devonshire might perhaps be interested? She
will have a very good portion, you know, and all those antiq-
uities must be expensive."

"No, I do not think that any of those gentlemen would appeal
to Eleanor. But I know someone who would!"

"Who? Tell me!" cried Lady Sefton.

Lady Jersey lowered her voice to whisper his name.

"You must be mad, Sally!" exclaimed her friend. "No, that
is really outside enough. I grant you that he is amusing
but . . . No, Sally, you must not!"

Lady Jersey made no comment, but there was a decidedly
wicked gleam in her shrewd, birdlike eyes.

"I wonder . . ." she murmured to herself. "I think I will. Yes, I really think I will. Shall you be at Almacks next week, my dear?"

"No, I cannot, I am afraid. Sefton wishes me to accompany him to Lincolnshire," answered Lady Sefton, a little warily.

"Well, I think that I will send Eleanor and the dear girls vouchers. It does not need us both to look after them. Do not worry, my dear."

"I am not worried, but I am afraid that you have some scheme in your head," answered Maria suspiciously.

"I?" exclaimed her ladyship, all innocence. "Why, my dear, not a scheme in the world other than to give my dearest friend's daughter a pleasant evening at our little club!"

chapter 5

Lady Jersey proved as good as her word. Within a very short space of time the promised vouchers had arrived. Emily and Harriet were in ecstasies. For years Almacks had been the dream of their lives. It was well known that a young lady had but to make an appearance at this fashionable club and instantly every eligible gentleman in England would fall madly in love with her. Of course Emily told herself that she did not care at all that any young man other than Simon would admire her, nevertheless she intended to look her very prettiest on this important evening. Nor was Eleanor impervious to the general excitement. To be returning to that center of the fashionable world from which she had been excluded so long! The prospect made her dizzy.

The rooms were almost overflowing that night for the season was in full swing. The club was crowded with debutantes, their formidable mamas, and the cream of the eligibles. Not for nothing was Almacks known as the marriage market.

Their party, honored for the first time by the dignified presence of Lord Portland, was greeted at once by Lady Jersey who bustled forward with a great rustling of silk to welcome as though they were her own personal guests. She bestowed a light embrace upon Eleanor and allowed his lordship to kiss her beringed hand before sweeping them off to the brightly lit ballroom. There she quickly presented each young lady with a partner and seemed about to perform the same office for Eleanor.

"Dear ma'am, do not trouble yourself, I beg," said Miss Portland hastily. "I assure you, I have no desire to dance."

"As you please, of course, my dear, but it seems quite ridiculous to me that a creature as lovely as yourself should be sitting out while so many plain little girls are dancing!" answered Lady Jersey with a shrug.

Eleanor could not be impervious to such flattery. She laughed and blushed, but still she refused to consider whirling around the room in company with her charges. Instead she moved gracefully to the seats reserved for the dowagers and seated herself, surveying the colorful scene with pleasure.

So far, thought Eleanor, she had been very fortunate for she had met nothing but kindness. She was aware that the mantle of protection which Lady Jersey's patronage had cast over her could not be relied upon completely. This visit to Almacks might indeed be regarded as a test. If she survived this evening without meeting any unpleasantness, then she might consider herself safe. She soon became aware, however, of a certain tension in the ladies sitting around her and so she held her head higher. She strove to appear oblivious to the whispering of two ladies in particular, one Mrs. Carruthers and her friend Lady Albemarle.

Lord Merriot, who had strolled into the rooms minutes before the doors closed at eleven, had entered a small alcove behind the sofa on which these women sat gossiping about Eleanor and the scandal with Lennox. He was enjoying a glass of excellent claret when his reverie was interrupted by Mrs. Carruthers's tuneless voice. He would have turned away in disgust if it had not become apparent that the subject of their conversation was the beautiful redheaded creature sitting so stiffly across from them. She had twice caught his interest before and so now he listened quite shamelessly to the story Mrs. Carruthers had to relate. He had been serving in His Majesty's Army when those dramatic events had shaken the *ton* and he had really no idea to whom he spoke when he had addressed Eleanor at Lady Sefton's soirée.

He glanced at her and it occurred to him that she seemed uncomfortable as she sat all alone. Acting upon a rare impulse of chivalry, he took Lady Jersey aside and murmured in her ear. She wrapped his knuckles with her fan, calling him a wicked creature, but nevertheless she made her way to Eleanor's chair.

"Here is a gentleman, my love, who begs that you will honor him with your hand," Lady Jersey said in a voice filled with laughter. "May I present Lord Merriot to you as a very desirable partner?"

Eleanor didn't know where to look. She flushed, averting her head, and in so doing she caught the malignant gaze of Mrs. Carruthers. She had no difficulty in reading that expression and her anger rose on the instant to meet the challenge. She extended her hand to Merriot. In a voice trembling with suppressed fury, she informed him she would be most happy to accept his kind offer.

The waltz was fast, requiring some dexterity, but he danced easily and without effort. She was well aware that more than one lady was following her progress with shocked eyes. The knowledge filled her with a reckless desire to give them even more to talk about. Lady Jersey had told her she must not hang her head and apologize to the world. Very well, then! She lifted her face to her partner and gave him a dazzling smile.

"I must thank you, sir, for giving me the opportunity to practice my steps. I learned to waltz only recently. It was not danced when I was previously in town," she told him with a glint in her eyes as he deftly twirled her around.

"I compliment you. No one would suspect it. You dance delightfully," he answered with his cool smile.

She wondered briefly whether he ever smiled with real warmth. Did that cold exterior mirror an equally icy heart?

As they danced, she caught many eyes upon them and she realized that he had noticed it too. Suddenly daring, she said in a challenging tone, "It is very brave of you to dance with a lady as notorious as I. Surely you must have heard by now that I am not at all the sort of person that you would wish to know!"

"On the contrary, from what I have heard of you, Miss Portland, you are precisely the sort of lady that I wish to know," he replied smoothly.

Eleanor gasped and cast a startled look at his impassive countenance. "I beg your pardon?" she said haughtily.

"Do not be so prickly, Miss Portland. I merely meant that I admire courage. You have that quality in abundance. However, if you will take my advice, you will not be so unguarded with strange gentlemen. Strive to appear unaware that you are the subject of impertinent gossip."

Eleanor did not know what to make of Merriot's admonition and heartily did she regret those foolish words of her own that had given him the opportunity to say such things to her. Having brought the subject into the conversation, she could hardly become offended when he followed her lead and spoke to her with such freedom.

He was regarding her rather sardonically, she thought, casting a glance into his handsome face from beneath her lashes. It was strange that he should have asked her to stand up with him, stranger still that she had accepted. She wondered suddenly if it were anger alone that had prompted her to do so. Had she not wanted to be in his arms? Had she not desired it since the first evening she had seen him at the York Assembly? All at once, she was desperately afraid. She could not allow herself to fall in love again and with such a man. His reputation was beyond repair. She knew him for a libertine, a gambler, even, if rumor did not lie, a killer! No, this must not be. In all probability, he had nothing more than a flirtation in mind or perhaps he sought to mount her as his latest mistress. Well, he would find himself very much mistaken if he took her for a light woman.

"May I ask why you are looking so very stern, Miss Portland?" he asked in an amused voice.

"Oh, was I? Forgive me, my lord, I was thinking of something else," she answered as coolly as he.

Lord Merriot was unused to ladies who allowed their minds to wander while he held them in his arms. It piqued him a little. Miss Portland had to be charmed out of her ill humor, for she was too beautiful a creature to be so indifferent to him.

"You must allow me to tell you, Miss Portland, that you take the shine out of every other woman here tonight. London is fortunate that you have returned to us. I wish that I had had the pleasure of knowing you during your previous visit. You must have been a very unusual young lady."

Eleanor flushed angrily. "Are you trying to insult me, sir?" she demanded.

"Good God, no!" he answered, dropping his lightly bantering tone. "How could you think so? I assure you, I would not do such a thing for the world!"

Eleanor could not believe him and surprisingly overset by this sudden contretemps she curtsied to her partner and fled to the sanctuary of the dowagers. She forced herself to sit calmly while inside she was shaking with anger and disappointment. Nor was Lord Merriot in any better state. He had certainly not intended to allude to the scandal of her past. Indeed he had almost forgotten it in the pleasure he felt in dancing with Eleanor.

Miss Portland was allowed very few moments in which to compose herself before she found her brother at her side in no pleasant mood.

"Where the devil have you been, Eleanor?" he demanded crossly.

"Only dancing, brother. Why?" she asked, surprised at his ill humor.

"May I remind you that you are in London principally to chaperone my daughter and not simply for your own enjoyment. Emily has disappeared and from what I can make out she has been gone this half hour and more!"

"Oh, no! Peter, I am so sorry. No wonder you are angry. It is too bad of her. Have you looked everywhere?" answered Eleanor penitently.

His lordship softened. "Well, I daresay there is no harm done. She is a thoughtless little puss and you are not much better yourself. However, I shall say no more about it if you can but find the child. God knows where she has got to!"

In fact, Emily was at that moment lifting her face to Simon's for their first kiss. It was a very gentle and rather a timid kiss for if truth be told it was the first time that Simon had ever held a girl in his arms. It was a heady sensation.

"Oh, Emily, dearest, sweetest Emily. How I love you," he breathed into the curls that were tickling his chin.

She snuggled her cheek into the hollow of his shoulder and thought that not in all the world was there another gentleman as noble, handsome, brave, and clever as her Simon. All of which was very satisfactory and just as it should be. Even Eleanor, when she eventually found them seated cosily upon a sofa far from the ballroom, had not the heart to be very stern with them. She thought they looked rather like a pair of very young puppies as they turned apprehensive brown eyes upon her.

She made a conscientious attempt to appear suitably annoyed.

"Simon, really! I had thought better of you than this. Consider what would have happened if you had been discovered by anyone other than myself. Emily would have been placed in a very awkward situation and there would have been a great deal of gossip to which I am sure you would not wish to expose my niece."

"I am sorry to contradict you, ma'am," answered Simon, very much on his dignity. "No one would dare to talk in such a way about my affianced wife."

"This is very sudden," commented Eleanor dryly. "Is this by any chance true, Emily? Have you indeed contracted an engagement without any reference to your papa? And you, Simon. Have you relayed the happy news to Viscount Lennox yet?"

Simon flushed. "No, ma'am, I have not," he answered sulkily.

"Then I think it would be as well if you did so before approaching my brother!" Her manner softened, for she saw that they were quite crushed by her severity. "My poor children. Never fear, I have done scolding. I only wish that my scoldings were the worst you will have to face. Go to your father, Simon, and tell him that you love Emily. Perhaps I am mistaken and all will go well with you, after all."

"You talk, Miss Portland, as though there is some great difficulty in the way of our marrying. Why should anyone object? It is not as though we were contemplating a *mésalliance*."

"I may be quite wrong, ask your father," was all that Eleanor could reply.

She returned her niece to the ballroom and informed her brother that she had found Emily dreaming upon a sofa. Which was in a way true but no mention was made of her companion.

It was growing late, but Emily's hand was sought for the remaining set and Harriet was still upon the floor with the faithful Montgomery. So Eleanor could not, as she longed to do, leave the ball for the sanctuary of her own bedchamber.

The memory of that dance with Merriot persisted in haunting her. Why had she said such a ridiculous thing to him? No

wonder he had responded with such a lack of respect. She
blushed at the thought. And had it not been for the well-known
fact that the claret cup served at Almacks was of the mildest,
she would have been much inclined to blame her odd behavior
on her indulgence in that innocuous beverage. She glanced
around the room. Merriot had left already, it seemed. Just as
well, Eleanor thought. She hoped very much that she might
never lay eyes upon his disturbing figure again! In view of this
wish, it was unfortunate that Lord Merriot should have decided
to call the very next morning in order to apologize for his words
the previous night.

Eleanor was quietly chuckling over the first chapters of
Pride and Prejudice when her visitor was announced.

Her first impulse was to deny herself, but she had caught
a glimpse of his lordship directly behind the butler and knew
that he must have seen her. She could not be so rude.

As Merriot entered the sunny morning room, it seemed to
shrink. He carried himself as always with his easy arrogance,
but she had not previously noted how powerful were his shoulders and strong athletic thighs. He was dressed for riding which
suited him and although Eleanor was quite unacquainted with
the magic name of Scott, she could not but see that his coat
fitted him as though molded to his form. For the rest, he
affected few dandyisms. His cravat was tied neatly, but was
not so high as to render turning his head a discomfort. He
carried a quizzing glass but used it rarely. He wore only one
ring, an antique signet of peculiar design. He looked every inch
of what he was—a Corinthian and a soldier. Yet there was
something in the lines of his rather hard countenance that gave
him a reckless, dissolute look. Eleanor could well understand
that some foolish women might find this very attractive. She,
of course, was far too sensible for any such silliness!

"It is kind of you to receive me, Miss Portland," he began
as he bowed over her hand. "I have come to offer my sincere
apologies for any words of mine that may have unwittingly,
I assure you, given offense."

Eleanor, although resolved against succumbing to the creature's attractions, could not but feel that it would be ungracious
to refuse such a handsome apology. "Thank you, sir," she
responded, a little stiffly. "I should have known that no gentleman would meaningly insult me by alluding to..."

He came to her rescue. "Believe me, ma'am, nothing was further from my mind. Should I ever be privileged by your confidence to talk of those events, I should describe you, not as unusual, but in my experience, unique!"

Eleanor was quite bewildered. Surely the man had not come here merely to insult her once more! What could he mean?

"In what way unique?" she demanded, ready for battle.

He smiled at her, a singularly warm, even affectionate smile. "Miss Portland, you were at Almacks last night. What did you see?"

She raised her eyebrows. "I saw a great many people dancing, sir. What else was there to see?"

"Forgive me, ma'am, but dancing was not the principal business of the evening. What you saw was an auction with all those pretty little girls in their white dresses for sale upon the block as surely as though they were black slaves. Virtuous, no doubt they are, few have had any opportunity to be anything else, but there is not one of them who has the courage to follow her heart and refuse to marry where Mama dictates. Her suitor may be old enough to be her grandfather, but if he has money he will get his little bride. He may be so debauched that his very touch will defile her but for the sake of a title he will be accepted. They are not forced into marriage, these charming young creatures, they are willing enough so long as they may have their pin money, their carriages, and often their lover too. But you... had the courage to say no to this ugly marriage market. You loved and loved passionately. And that is why I say that you are unique, Miss Portland!"

Not unnaturally, Eleanor was considerably taken aback. She knew not what to make of her surprising guest, but somehow her intuition told her that he was speaking to her out of personal bitterness and she could not but pity him.

"Sir, I do not know how to answer you," she said softly.

He seemed about to speak again, but they were interrupted by the sudden sound of angry voices in the hallway outside the door. There were loud, angry tones from the men, and above them the sound of heartbroken sobbing. All at once, Eleanor jumped up, her visitor quite forgotten. "Why, it is Lucy crying, I am sure of it!" She flung open the doors and gasped in dismay at the sight which met her eyes.

Lucy was hanging, half carried, half dragged, between the butler Fiskin and another man. She was pleading with them in a hysterical voice but was commanded to keep quiet by Mrs. Burrows, the grim-faced housekeeper. It was she who was directing operations. As Eleanor approached, she dropped a curtsy.

"Forgive all the noise, ma'am. This wicked girl would insist on trying to see you before she left the house. I told her and told her she could not but in the end she ran up here and, as you see, she won't leave without us making her!"

Eleanor was aghast. "But, Good God, what is the meaning of this? Whatever has she done that you should treat her so?"

"I just discovered, ma'am, that the little tart has been carrying on with some fellow and now she has gone and got herself in the family way, if you'll pardon the expression, ma'am."

Lucy broke away from her captors and threw herself upon the floor in front of Eleanor. "Oh, miss, miss, please don't let them send me away. I've nowhere to go and what's to become of me out there on the streets with a baby comin'? I'll die, miss, if they sends me away!"

Eleanor bent over the sobbing girl and laid a protective arm across her shoulders. "Lucy, my poor child. Can you not go to the father of your baby? Surely he will help you?"

"No, miss, I can't, 'cause he's married already!" declared Lucy, weeping bitterly.

Eleanor gasped as though she had been struck. Lord Merriot, who had been watching the scene with interest, noted that she had turned terribly pale. He judged it time to take a hand in the scene.

"May I be of assistance, Miss Portland?" he drawled, surveying the housekeeper through his glass with some disfavor.

"Thank you, my lord, but there is nothing more to be done. Lucy will remain in this house until I say that she is to go," Eleanor informed the housekeeper angrily. "She is to be given only light work such as dusting and sewing. If I find that she has suffered unkindness at the hands of anyone in this household, then it is that person who will be turned out of the house, not Lucy. Do I make myself clear?"

The housekeeper withdrew in some disorder, leaving the stately butler to explain that it had been her doing entirely and nothing to do with him. Eleanor cut short these excuses and sent the rest of the gaping servants away with a few well-chosen words.

Lord Merriot, an appreciative spectator to all this, was heard to murmur to himself as he quietly left the house, "Yes, unique, really quite unique!"

chapter 6

It was the freely expressed opinion of the household that Miss Portland had run mad. To be defending the miserable Lucy was bad enough, and not what was to be expected from the quality, but to actually keep her in the house with two young ladies living there! Utterly incomprehensible.

To Lucy, of course, Eleanor appeared in the light of a goddess come down from heaven to save her.

"Oh, miss, I've been such a bad girl," sobbed the little maidservant, as later that day she sat in Eleanor's bedchamber pouring out her woeful tale. "I knows I shouldn't 'ave done it, but it didn't seem like it was wrong or bad then. It was just natural-like. Only later, when I thought what me old mum would 'ave said to me, then I felt real bad. Do you think she can see, miss? Do you think she knows what I done and is sorry for it?"

Eleanor laid a gentle hand upon her head. "Lucy, I do not know if the dead watch the living, but I do know this. Your mother loved you in life and she does not love you any less now. If she sees you then, you may be sure she understands and forgives."

"Oh, miss, do you really think so? That makes me feel ever so much better. It can't be really wrong, can it, when I love 'im so. I'm goin' to love my baby too and do my best for him, poor little bas——" she stopped abruptly.

"Love child?" suggested Eleanor with a smile.

"Aye, 'e's that all right!" responded Lucy with a giggle.

"Your feelings are very right, Lucy, I know you will always do your duty toward your child. But you know, Lucy, I cannot think that it will be comfortable for you in this house where everyone knows your story. I do not wish to pry but it must be that you will meet the father, whoever he is, if you remain here and that will not be good for either of you."

Lucy nodded. "Oh, aye, 'e'll be around again and I know I shouldn't see 'im but I don't think I'd 'ave the heart to say no. But there ain't no place else for me to go!"

"Perhaps I could send you down to the country," said Eleanor thoughtfully. It occurred to her, however, that her sister-in-law would hardly welcome the girl in her condition. Where else could she go? A wild hope darted into her brain. Lord Merriot, she knew, had huge estates in the north somewhere. Could she persuade him to provide for Lucy? If he admired her as much as he seemed to, perhaps he would be happy to oblige her in this affair. It was a pleasant thought. She fell to thinking of Merriot. Lucy's troubles had temporarily driven his strange words from her head, but now she savored them again. He actually admired her for her reprehensible conduct, thought her courageous and unusual. How odd. But then he was a puzzling man. She had been told all manner of dreadful things about him, but they seemed to bear little relation to the man she knew. He might be a libertine, but he had shown no sign of wishing to make love to her. She wondered why not and was shocked to find herself slightly put out that he had made no such attempt. As for the other accusations, she could not judge, never having seen him at cards. Altogether, she could not help thinking that very likely his sins had been much exaggerated.

"Do not worry yourself, Lucy. I will think of something," she assured the girl. Now go along to your room and rest. You are far too pale!"

Lucy departed reluctantly for she was not anxious to quit the protection of Eleanor's presence. However, their mistress's words had so powerfully affected the rest of the staff that they treated Lucy with a respect bordering upon servility, a most welcome change for the little maidservant.

Eleanor was left alone to compose a suitable note to Lord Merriot, a task she found unexpectedly difficult. She wished to consult him upon a question that no lady should know anything about. Moreover, she was well aware that should he agree to give Lucy shelter on his estates, the censorious world would draw its own conclusions. From what she had seen of Merriot she did not think that the opinion of the world that he had fathered a bastard upon a pretty abigail would bother him in the least.

In the end, she dispatched a short note begging his lordship to do her the favor of calling upon her the next day if convenient.

To Eleanor's surprise, she was to receive yet another visitor this trying day. Four o'clock in the afternoon was an unusual hour for making calls and so she looked up in some astonishment when Lady Sefton was ushered into the room.

Her visitor seemed conscious that her appearance was untimely and yet she was strangely loath to come to the point. Eleanor politely offered her guest tea, which was accepted. For some half hour they chatted upon commonplace matters when suddenly Lady Sefton appeared to gather her courage together and quite out of the blue she said, "I believe that Merriot was here this morning, Eleanor?"

"Yes, ma'am. Lord Merriot did me the honor to pay me a morning call," answered Eleanor, a little stiffly.

"Oh, dear!" exclaimed her visitor distressfully. "Eleanor, I am dreadfully to blame! It was in my house that you met the man and now see what has come of it!"

"So far as I am aware, nothing has 'come of it,' Lady Sefton," replied Eleanor with deceptive calm. "I am very far from understanding you."

"Pray, do not be so stiff and cold, for it shows that the man has already won you over. It is as I feared! Eleanor, please believe me, you must have nothing more to do with Merriot. It is not safe for you!"

"Do you doubt me, ma'am? Do you think my virtue so easily overcome because once it was? I do not think that I deserve that."

Lady Sefton was almost in tears. "But you do not understand. Merriot has so bad a reputation that if you smile at him half London will believe you are already his mistress. And you have waltzed with the creature and received him here alone! Oh, how could you be so imprudent?"

"Lady Sefton, are you not exaggerating a little?" demanded Eleanor in a reasonable tone. "After all, Lady Jersey herself presented Lord Merriot to me."

"Sally Jersey has no more sense than a peahen," declared her old friend roundly. "Why, I could recount the names of a dozen women that Merriot has ruined. Poor Sophia Wrexham left her husband and two children to run off with him and he tired of her within a twelvemonth. Then there was Charlotte Preston. She went into a decline and very nearly died when the wretch deserted her. If you encourage his attentions who will believe you innocent?"

Eleanor raised her head, which she had lowered, that Lady Sefton should not see her tears. "Am I to have no friends, then? Am I to be forever barred from normal human intercourse because of past mistakes? And Merriot, too. No doubt it was very wicked of him to seduce these ladies but is he wholly to blame? Did he kidnap this Sophia Wrexham or did she go with him willingly? You say he tired of her. What makes you so sure? Perhaps it was the other way round. There are such women!"

Lady Sefton sighed. "It is of no use talking to you, my dear. You are in love with him already. I am too late."

Eleanor opened her lips to deny the charge, but somehow she could not. Could Lady Sefton be right?

"Eleanor, forgive me, but I know what I am talking about. Please think very carefully before you give the world further cause to gossip about the two of you," said Lady Sefton as she rose to leave. "I should be so sorry if the splendid new start that you have made here were to be spoiled by yet more scandal!"

Eleanor could not be angry with her kind friend but the knowledge that once more disaster threatened had the undesirable effect of making her all the more determined to pursue her friendship with Merriot. She could hardly contain herself until she was able to demonstrate to the watching *ton* that she cared less than nothing for them or for their opinion of her.

It was in this defiant mood that she made ready to go to the opera that evening. It was a treat for which her charges were less than enthusiastic, their only hope for the evening being the possibility that Simon or Lord Montgomery might be among the crowd. All three ladies had reason therefore to dress with unusual care.

They were set down outside the magnificent Opera House in Covent Garden among a fashionable throng. As it happened, Eleanor had never attended the opera during her first season and so was quite as overcome as the girls by the size and style of the establishment.

Very few of the assembled *ton* had come to the theater because of any great love of music. They had come to see and be seen and most were now engaged in surveying the boxes through their opera glasses, bowing to any notables present.

Eleanor was by now in the fortunate position of being able to exchange nods and smiles with a good many ladies. This gratifying circumstance greatly added to her enjoyment of the very mediocre entertainment being offered.

The first act seemed incredibly tedious to the girls who were anxious for the interval during which the real business of the evening would be conducted. Each was hopeful that their box would be visited nor, if truth were told, was Eleanor as indifferent to the prospect as she would have liked to appear. She was forced to admit to herself that she very much wanted to see Merriot again and could not help remembering Lady Sefton's words. But of course the idea was absurd. One did not fall in love in a matter of days. At least not when one had reached the great age of seven-and-twenty.

The interminable act closed at last and the house rose as with one mind. Ladies waved discreetly to their cavaliers, beaus raked the boxes through their glasses and quizzed any shy Beauties that their fancy lit upon, and even genuine music lovers decided to take a turn in the galleries outside the auditorium where cool lemonade might be obtained.

"Look, Harry!" cried Emily. "There is Montgomery. He has seen us! Oh, I am sure he will come up to pay his respects. Do take off your spectacles, Harriet. There is not the least need of them now!" Harriet blushed furiously but did as she was bid. Montgomery, who was by no means as sure of himself as his friend, took a little time to summon up his courage but he did at last appear and Harriet's shy smile soon reassured him. He begged that he might have the honor of remaining in their box for the rest of the performance and as this was quite the established mode the ladies agreed. Eleanor and Emily, however, were to be disappointed and were still searching the house for their admirers when the performance recommenced.

Had there been no second interval to look forward to, it is doubtful whether Emily could have been persuaded to sit through the second act which she pronounced even drearier than the first. Indeed Eleanor, too, found it difficult to concentrate upon the drama, so busy was she in planning what she should say to Merriot when she saw him and how she could demonstrate satisfactorily to the world that she intended to be friends with anyone she chose. Meanwhile, although it wasn't absolutely certain, it seemed extremely likely that Lord Montgomery held Harriet's hand throughout.

During the next break, Eleanor decided that she was quite tired of sitting in the stuffy box and ushered her little party outside where they could stroll about and obtain some refreshment. The galleries were crowded but a man as tall as Merriot was easily detected and they had not been walking up and down for more than five minutes when Eleanor saw his elegant head above the crowd. He was moving toward her and she began to blush a little, thinking that he must have seen her. It was not until he was almost directly upon them that she saw his companion. Leaning upon his arm in a most possessive manner was a luscious Beauty to whom he was listening in a most attentive way as she murmured to him and cast languishing glances at him from under her sooty lashes.

Eleanor was by no means the only person to be struck by this handsome couple. Indeed they caused a small sensation as they passed, for the lady was clad in a gown so diaphanous as to leave very little to the imagination. Eleanor indignantly suspected that her petticoats had been damped to insure just that sensuous clinging.

As they reached Eleanor, Merriot happened to raise his eyes from the enchanting face at his side. For a moment he gazed straight into Eleanor's burning eyes. What he saw there gave him a moment's pause. It seemed as though he would speak but instead he gave a slight bow and passed on. A little buzz of conversation arose in their wake.

"Mark my words, Amanda will go too far one of these days! That dress was positively indecent," Eleanor heard one lady exclaim to another.

"Oh, I know, but you must own she looks magnificent.

They say he is still passionately in love with her. Quite a triumph to have attached Merriot!"

"My love, I would give my ears to be in her place," answered the other frankly.

They moved away, but Eleanor had heard enough. So Merriot was in love with that exotic creature. Well, it was only to be expected. How could she have been silly enough to indulge herself in foolish dreams?

"Aunt Eleanor, did you see that lovely woman?" demanded Emily, breaking in upon her thoughts. "She was with the gentleman you waltzed with at Almacks. I have found out all about her. She is the Lady Amanda Montclair and her husband is very old. Montgomery says that she has been Merriot's mistress for ages. I should think he would be in love with her, would not you? She is so very beautiful!"

Miss Portland felt that she had borne enough. She rounded on the surprised Emily, saying sternly, "I can only wonder at your indelicacy, Emily, in talking of such matters which you should know nothing about. As for Lord Montgomery, I had thought better of him. I shall certainly tell him that if he wishes to associate with Harriet it would be better if he would refrain from entertaining her with tap-room gossip!"

This withering speech not unnaturally brought tears to Emily's soft brown eyes. Her aunt was not usually so nice in matters of gossip for they had enjoyed many agreeable sessions since they came to London pulling to pieces the reputations of various ladies whose haughtiness had provoked them. She would have spoken hotly in her own defense had not Harriet kicked her sharply on the shin.

"Ouch! What did you do that for?" she demanded, aggrieved.

"Hush!" commanded Harriet, dragging her away from her aunt. "Emily, you must not say anything to Miss Portland. Can you not see that she is not herself?" she hissed in an urgent whisper.

"I do not have the slightest idea what you are talking about," replied Emily crossly.

"Sometimes you are quite blind, Emily! Did you not notice how Lord Merriot stared at her that first time in the Park? And later she danced with him when she had said positively that she would not dance with anyone."

"I still do not see why that should make her so disagreeable," responded Emily with a shrug.

Harriet smiled mysteriously. "Silly! Why, you told me the story yourself. Do you not see? I believe that Merriot is the man she ran away with all those years ago!"

Emily gasped in astonishment. "Harry, do you really think so? I must say it's a very good notion. But he was supposed to be married. I do not think that there is a Lady Merriot."

"There may have been. Perhaps he is a widower. Oh, just think how lovely it would be if they were to fall in love all over again. This time there is nothing to stop them marrying. Is it not romantic?"

Needless to say, Eleanor would have been horrified had she had the smallest notion of this misconception. She was, however, quite pale and tense enough to lend the assertion some color. She could not prevent herself from occasionally glancing toward his box, nor did the sight help her to regain her composure.

The couple sat together, far closer than common acquaintance dictated. He had often to bend his handsome head to hear his lovely companion's whispers, whispers which Eleanor did not for a moment believe were comments upon the performance.

If Eleanor had been able to hear those intimate murmurings her heart would have been lightened considerably. Amanda, who had not failed to notice that burning exchange of looks, was being rather tiresome.

"Who was that woman? Why does she keep looking at us?" she demanded in a low but querulous tone.

"That *lady*," answered Merriot, laying emphasis upon the word, "is a very kind and gracious acquaintance for whom I have considerable respect."

She would have been wiser to leave well enough alone but she was too jealous to be reasonable. "Respect indeed! I pity her then for from the looks of her it is more than respect that she wants from you, Robert. Why, the way she looks at you is indecent!"

"As distinct from your own looks, I suppose?" he answered, nettled.

She gave a titter. "Good God, I hope I do not look so lovelorn. I am no aging spinster!"

They were obliged to cease their quarrel as their neighbors

indicated that they had come to listen to the opera, not to their bickering. Merriot was, however, more seriously displeased with Amanda than he had been in all the months of their association.

He had never been in love with her but her tantalizing beauty had satisfied his senses and her wit had occasionally entertained him. Now, however, he discovered she had a strain of vulgarity that disgusted him. She was displaying far too much possessiveness. He had never led her to believe she was more to him than she was, but lately he had been wondering whether it would not be wiser to break off their relationship.

Later that night as he waited for her in the scented boudoir, he found that he was looking forward to their lovemaking with far less than his usual anticipation. She was an exciting creature, experienced and demanding, but tonight he did not desire that soft yielding body which once had inflamed him so. His thoughts turned instead to a tall elegant figure whose vivid hair and haunted eyes had begun to trouble his dreams a little. Wondering how it would feel to hold her, slender and firm, in his arms, he felt desire stir within him. She would be passionate, he knew, if only he could awaken that passion. But it was not only her body he wanted. He suddenly knew that he longed to drive out that hurt look from her lovely eyes, to warm her with his love. Love! He must be mad. Surely he had given up such mawkishness long ago!

The door opened and the very different figure of Amanda appeared before him. She had changed her clinging muslins for an even more transparent robe of floating sea-green chiffon. Her luxuriant hair fell to her waist, caressing her smooth bare shoulders. Beneath the thin stuff of her garment he could see her ripe body, scented with roses and smooth with softening oils. She approached him languorously, sure of her power, and stood before him, allowing him to admire her to the full, before she descended softly into his arms and twined her own round his neck. His embrace enfolded her automatically, his lips found hers softly inviting, and at first he hoped that he might ease the hunger he felt by possessing her. His kisses were demanding and she answered him as passionately, pressing her warm body against him, uttering tiny groans of pleasure deep in her throat. She took his hands and pressed them to her full breasts and as he caressed them she sought with her own white hands to unfasten the ivory studs on his shirt. As her hands

touched his flesh he realized that whatever happened between
Eleanor and himself she had spoiled forever his pleasure in this
joyless coupling. He could not make love to this rapacious
woman.

Abruptly he pulled away, leaving her gasping, her gown
falling about her breasts, her eyes and lips heavy with passion.

"Robert, what is it?" she demanded, almost frightened by
the expression on his face.

"Forgive me, Amanda, but I cannot stay! I must go," he
told her, awkward as a schoolboy.

"Go!" she shrieked. "Go where, you fool!"

He pulled himself together. "Amanda, my sweet, I am truly
sorry, but delightful although our relationship has been, I am
afraid it must end. You are in every way everything that a man
could desire, the fault is with me. Come, my dear, I do not
flatter myself that I am the only man in your life nor that you
will mourn for me very long."

Such a thing had never happened to her ladyship before.
Always it had been she who had grown bored, she who dismissed her lovers. Certainly, it was true that he shared the
privilege with several gentlemen, with the notable exception
of her husband, but he could not cast her off like this! She
picked up the nearest object, which happened to be a priceless
Sèvres vase and flung it at his head. He ducked and it shattered
harmlessly against the door. Several more articles followed it,
but the only one that actually found its mark was a heavy brass
candlestick which caught him on the temple causing a trickle
of blood to run down his cheek. He was laughing now, thankful
that the scene had switched from high drama to low comedy.
"No more, my dear, I beg!" he cried, holding out his hands
to ward off further missiles. "Let us part friends, Amanda.
Admit that you were growing bored with me in any event."

Amanda deigned no answer to this rather typically male
attempt to justify his behavior, but threw herself upon the sofa
and burst into hysterical tears. Merriot paused, concerned, but
believing that her tears had more to do with anger and hurt
pride than with any real distress, he left her there and let himself
quietly out of the house.

As the door closed, Amanda sat up abruptly. He had been
very near the truth when he had said that she was growing tired
of the affair. He was a magnificent lover but Amanda craved
novelty and although he had satisfied her appetites for almost

a year, she would not be loath to find a new interest. Her real distress had a far more practical source. Merriot was by far the wealthiest of her lovers to date and Amanda was very expensive. Her husband, although generous enough in most respects, flatly refused to pay his wife's gaming debts for he disapproved of women who gambled. Merriot had no such inconvenient scruples nor had he been at all shocked at the amount of her obligations. His purse had been readily opened to pay off debts for his mistress who had not now the slightest idea how she was to find the money to pay off creditors who were becoming daily more pressing in their demands.

Lord Merriot, striding down the street, blood still congealed upon his lean cheek, was conscious of an elation that he could not remember experiencing since he was a green youth of twenty. He had received Eleanor's stiff note and had already formed the intention of calling but not for the purpose that Eleanor had in mind. How one could delicately convey to a lady that one had broken with one's mistress for her sake, he was not at all sure, but he would do it and then set himself to winning the only woman who had been able to stir his blood like this for more years than he cared to remember. In an uncharacteristically romantic gesture, he made his way through Grosvenor Square to South Audley Street and stood for a moment before what he fancied to be Eleanor's widow. He kissed his hand to the house and strolled away curiously happy and at peace with himself.

chapter 7

The following morning was fine and bright, encouraging a gentleman making his way down South Audley Street to dispense with his drab greatcoat and to sport instead a coat of olive-green superfine. He walked briskly enough in the chill morning air but there was that in his manner that suggested that his errand was not a happy one. His handsome face was frowning slightly and tension betrayed itself in the tightly clenched fist. He arrived at last at the house he sought and halted for a moment as though nerving himself for the ordeal ahead.

Fiskin, when he opened the door to this early visitor, recognized him at a glance. The butler had served in too many great houses not to know that the Viscount Lennox was a welcome guest among the highest in the land.

"Good morning," began the Viscount, ever courteous. "Will you be so good as to convey my card to Miss Portland." Fiskin was a little shocked but impressed. No doubt it would have been more proper had the visitor demanded his lordship but that gentleman had already left for his club and neither of Eleanor's charges had yet made an appearance. It ill suited the butler's notions of propriety to usher this important but personable guest into his mistress's presence, but he bowed and took the card.

Eleanor was in the morning room picking at what seemed to her a singularly unappetizing breakfast. She had dressed in one of her old gowns, too dispirited to make an effort over her appearance. Had she but known it, the gown of soft turquoise muslin with its neatly ruffled neck and long tight sleeves became her admirably. Despite its shabbiness, her hair shone more brightly, her skin seemed whiter, and her magnificent figure had never looked so fine.

She took the elegant white card that Fiskin proffered and glanced idly at the flowing copperplate. She turned pale and sat up with a gasp.

"Oh, I . . . I . . . cannot see . . . Surely his lordship wishes to talk to my brother, not me!" she stammered incoherently.

"No, miss, the gentleman asked quite plainly for Miss Portland. I told him that my lord was not at home," replied Fiskin with an injured air.

"Oh! Well . . . er . . . perhaps you had best show his lordship into the blue salon. I will see him there," said Eleanor with an effort.

The butler bowed and withdrew. Eleanor, left alone, pressed her cold hands to her burning cheeks in an effort to cool them. She had rarely felt so agitated. What could the man want with her? She had almost forgotten to think about the Viscount of late, so quickly had Merriot ousted him from her thoughts. Nevertheless she was not so completely indifferent to Lennox that she could contemplate this private interview without distress. She moved to the mirror and attempted to smooth her unruly curls. The woman she saw reflected there was a poor creature, she thought. She gave herself an encouraging smile and lifted her chin.

Lennox waited for her with similar feelings. Only the most urgent necessity had prompted him to seek this meeting. Eleanor was unaware of the fact, but Lennox had been deliberately avoiding her, never attending any function where there was a chance that she might appear. He did not trust himself in her presence and was determined not to allow her to complicate his life once more.

He had been pleasantly surprised the previous evening when Simon had scratched his door and begged for a moment to speak with him alone. He had been happy to see his son and, although on the point of departing to spend the evening with his latest mistress, had invited the boy to take a glass of port with him.

"Thank you, sir, I should like a little," Simon had replied, for he was rather nervous.

"Here you are, my boy. Sip it slowly for it is excellent wine. I remember my father putting it down thirty years ago."

Fearing that his father might embark on even more reminiscences, a habit to which he was prone and which his offspring deplored, Simon quickly interrupted. "Father, I have something very important to say. Something which affects my whole future!"

"Well, my boy. Say it, then," had answered his lordship, amused by this vehemence.

"The thing is . . . Well, I am thinking . . . I want to get married!" stammered Simon, blushing like a schoolboy.

"This is very sudden." The Viscount smiled. "May I inquire who the young lady might be?"

"Oh, you have met her, sir. You remember that day in the Park when I introduced you to Miss Portland. Well, it's her niece Emily. Oh, Father, she is the dearest, sweetest girl in the world! I love her so much and she loves me too. You must have been struck when you saw her. So much sweetness combined with such loveliness. We have been in love ever since we first met in York. There can be no objection. Her father is Lord Portland and she is his only child."

"You are mistaken, Simon," interrupted his father. "There is every objection!"

Simon stared at his father in amazement. "What on earth do you mean, sir?" he demanded.

Lennox had paled. He looked different, quite unlike his usual easygoing self. "I am not willing to go into long explanations, Simon. I will only say that I am not prepared to countenance any connection between you and a member of that particular family. Is that clearly understood?"

Simon was a good-hearted boy who seldom set up his will in opposition to his parents, but this arbitrary command was too much for him. "Good God, sir! Do you really believe that I am going to give up the girl I love just like that, without a word? Without any reason given? I hope I am too much your son for such behavior. I have pledged myself to Emily and I am bound to her as much by honor as by my feelings for her. I will not break my word for you or for any other man!"

Under any other circumstances Lennox would have been proud of his son for this defiance, but on this issue he was not reasonable. Instead he made the mistake of presenting his only child with an ultimatum. The youth must give up Emily or face disinheritance!

"Sir, you could not!" cried Simon aghast. "It is not as though I wanted to marry some opera dancer or actress. Emily is unexceptionable!"

"You have heard all I am prepared to say on the matter," answered his father coldly.

They stared at each other for a long moment and then without a word the boy turned on his heel and left the room.

It was this interview that had brought the Viscount to see Eleanor. He had spoken in anger and had no real intention of cutting Simon off but neither could he bear to contemplate the consequences that such a marriage would inevitably bring. He decided that he had best consult Eleanor who was no doubt as well aware of the dangers as he was himself.

So lost in thought was he that he did not hear Eleanor enter the room and it was a shock when she addressed him in her cool pleasant voice.

"Good morning, Lord Lennox."

He looked up quickly. It seemed to him she had not changed at all during the long years. Then he noticed there was a calm composure about her that had not been there before. She had matured but she was every bit as desirable as she had been that first morning when he had held her, trembling and faint in his supporting arms.

She gave him a formal curtsey, but she did not offer her hand. "Will you not be seated, my lord," she said politely. "I believe that you have something to say to me?"

"Miss Portland . . . Eleanor . . ."

"Miss Portland will do very well, my lord!"

He bowed. "I beg your pardon, ma'am. I have something of importance to discuss with you. If I should inadvertently conjure up memories as painful to me as to yourself then you will, I hope, forgive me."

"I shall try, sir. I find that forgiveness is something I have practiced a good deal in the past few years. The only person to whom I cannot extend it is myself!"

He winced a little but pulled himself together enough to say, "You are generous. Do you think that I have found it easy to forgive myself? I promise you that I did not!"

She made a little gesture as though begging him to stop. "Whatever you wanted to say to me, sir, I am sure that you did not come here simply to tell me this!"

"Naturally not," he answered in an annoyed tone.

"Then what do you want?"

"My son," he answered baldly.

"I do not have him!" she snapped.

Lennox nodded. "True enough, ma'am. However, your niece is more fortunate. Eleanor . . . I beg your pardon, Miss Portland, you must be aware, as I am, that nothing but misery can result from this marriage. Too many people know what happened between us. There will be gossip, the whole scandal will be revived. What sort of basis is that for two young people to start their life together?"

"I can remember a time, my lord, when scandal did not seem too great a price to pay. I cannot think that Simon and Emily will have less courage. They love each other very truly, I think."

The sight of her coolly reproving him, so lovely and so unattainable, maddened him. "I see what it is! You had this planned from the start. This is your revenge upon me!" he flung at her. "Could you not forgive me for leaving you? For doing my best to forget you all these years? Very well, punish me but for God's sake do not take Simon away from me. Let him go!"

She rose, pale with fury. "How dare you! How dare you take that righteous tone with me? I do not think you care at all what happens to those two young people. It is nothing but selfishness. You do not want to have to see me, to be reminded every day that you ruined me and then abandoned me to whatever punishment my family could devise! Have you never thought of how I spent those ten years? Have you never wondered whether that brief union bore fruit?"

He sprang up and strode across the room. He grabbed her by the shoulders and shook her unmercifully, shouting, "It's a lie. Damn you, say it is a lie. Tell me you are lying. There was no child!"

She laughed harshly. "No, Richard. There was no child!"

He released her and sat down abruptly, his head clasped in

his hands. His attitude recalled to her the evening when she had come upon him unaware, struggling with his unhappiness. But now she felt no particular desire to comfort him. She regarded him with a detached kind of pity. "Do not be distressed, Richard. I have suffered but it is over now. All I ask is that you leave me alone to build a new life!"

"How can I? Do you not see that if Simon marries Emily we shall have to meet again and again? How could we stand it? We could not help but become lovers once more. Can you not see how much I want you even now?"

"I am sorry for that, Lennox, but I fear that it is your problem. You see I do not feel any desire to renew our relationship. In fact, I can think of nothing that I should like less!"

She was not being deliberately cruel, she merely intended to make herself quite clear. She might as well have spared her breath, however, as Lennox's vanity would not allow him to believe her. Exasperatingly, he smiled at her as though he quite understood her feelings and did not intend to embarrass her. Instead he bowed and prepared to leave her.

"Will you speak to Emily?" he asked as they moved toward the door.

"No," she answered quietly. "I fail to see why my niece should be made unhappy simply because you and I were once indiscreet. But I shall try to explain to her why you oppose the match. It is unfair that she should believe that you dislike her for her own sake. If I were you I should tell Simon. Emily is bound to do so in any event and I think that it would be better coming from you."

"It would be of little use begging you not to tell her, I suppose?" he asked in a hopeless tone.

"If you continue to forbid the marriage, there is nothing else I can do, Richard. I will not have Emily made more unhappy than she need be. I do not think that I owe you more loyalty than I owe to that child."

"You have changed," he told her. "I did not think at first that you had but now I see. You have no pity left in you."

"You are mistaken, Lennox. I do feel pity, but not for you nor for myself. We do not deserve it!"

They exchanged one long, bitter look, then Lennox turned on his heel and abruptly left the room.

Finding herself once more alone, Eleanor sank into a chair utterly exhausted. She was trembling and in a detached sort of way she wondered why. It had been a terrible effort to remain calm, to prevent herself from hurling at his head all the pent-up anger within her, but she knew that it would not be fair. He had always been weaker than she. That foolish flight had been her fault. She acknowledged that. What she found impossible to forgive was that long silence. He had convinced himself that she was happy enough locked away with her family in the Yorkshire countryside. That was like him. He wished it to be so and in his mind it was so. She sighed. It was never pleasant to look back on love and curse oneself for a fool!

She was not to be left alone long to indulge her depression. Fiskin interrupted her once again. This time he brought the expected visitor. Merriot had arrived.

He entered the room eagerly, bringing with him the vigor and brightness of the outside world. She smiled at him more warmly than she had intended, so happy was she to see him again.

"Miss Portland! Are you ill?" he demanded, shocked to see her so pale.

She forebore to inform him that she had not only passed a sleepless night for his sake but also had just sustained a shattering interview with her former lover. Instead she made the usual polite disclaimer.

"I am quite well, just a little tired, my lord," she told him in a wan voice.

"But this will not do at all!" he exclaimed. "Tell me, do you think that a drive in my curricle would refresh you? I came to ask if you would care to drive out to Dulwich with me. The new gallery has just opened, you know. They say that it is very fine and the drive is through some pretty countryside."

She smiled at him with real gratitude.

"I should like that excessively. Will you allow me ten minutes to change and to tell the girls that I am going out?"

"Of course." He bowed. "Take as long as you need."

As it happened, she did not keep him waiting above half an hour. Emily and Harriet, who were engaged with several other young ladies to walk in Kensington Gardens, were only too happy to dispense with Eleanor's chaperonage and sent her off with hearty good will. She appeared before his lordship in an elegantly cut driving dress of dark blue velvet worn with a little fur-trimmed jacket and a jaunty bonnet.

"May I say that you look charming, Miss Portland," he told

her, the look in his eyes giving the formal words an added meaning.

"Thank you, sir," she answered demurely. "Oh, what a beautiful team!" she exclaimed as they descended to the pavement. "I have never seen such a well-matched pair!"

"You care for horses, Miss Portland?" he asked as they drove expertly through the crowded streets toward the river.

"Oh, indeed, I do. I was used to drive myself everywhere until . . ."

"Until?" he prompted gently.

"Until my father decided that I was not to be trusted with . . . his horses," she replied with an effort.

His lordship was silent for a moment. "Would you care to take the reins now?" he asked politely.

She laughed. "Oh, my lord, how disconcerted you would be if I said yes. I was the veriest whipster even then and I have not driven for more than ten years. But it was kind of you to suggest it!"

He joined in her laughter. "It was the only way that suggested itself to me of telling you how very much the pleasure of your company means to me."

For the past few moments she had forgotten the shadow that lay between them but now the vision of Amanda Montclair arose before her and she answered in a strained voice.

"Your lordship is fortunate in being acquainted with so many ladies whose company gives you pleasure."

Abruptly Merriot halted the carriage. Turning to the groom who sat impassively behind them he said, "Wilkins. Do you think that you can find your way home from here?"

"Aye, sir," answered the man laconically.

"Here is a guinea for you. Do so," instructed Merriot briefly.

"Good God, my lord, what are you doing?" demanded Eleanor as the man jumped down.

He turned to her with a singularly charming smile. "My dear Miss Portland, I have a great deal to say to you. I do not wish for an audience."

"What do you mean?" she asked, suddenly fearful. Was he going to make her a proposition? And, treacherous thought, what would she answer if he did?

"Miss Portland, I want to tell you a story. The story of a rather foolish young man. Will you listen to me?" he asked as the carriage once more rolled forward through the lanes of Chelsea.

She turned her head to study his handsome profile. "I should like to hear your story, my lord."

"Very well, then. This young man was a younger son and rather a bad lot, I am afraid. He caused his mother a great deal of heartbreak, but he was not vicious, I believe, only wild. He was destined to become a soldier. The year that he donned his regimentals for the first time he became acquainted with a girl. Her name is not important now but she was very, very lovely and unfortunately very stupid as well. Naturally I . . . or rather my hero, did not notice the lack of brains, he was far too taken by her pretty face and naive ways. In short he fell madly in love with her. And she returned his love, so far as she was capable."

"Are you not a little cruel to her, sir?" interposed Eleanor. "She must have been very young."

"She was just seventeen, as you were when you fell in love. In any event they exchanged vows unbeknownst to her parents or his. He went off to fight in the Peninsula and when he returned a year later on leave, it was to find her betrothed to a man three times her age."

"Poor boy," said Miss Portland softly.

He smiled at her. "Many would have said 'poor girl,' but you are right, it was he who should be pitied. She was happy enough in contemplation of the wealth that she would enjoy. Until, that is, he returned to remind her of their vows. Suddenly the money seemed less important to her. She became unhappy and when he urged her to fly with him she agreed. They arranged a rendezvous, only a few steps for her. Then they would fly to Gretna. Romantic, is it not?"

She made no answer, but her hands were clasped so tightly that her nails dug into her palms.

"Well, he waited several hours and not entirely in vain. She did not keep their appointment, but her brothers and her father did and inflicted a beating upon her lover which kept him on his back for a week. Doubtless in their eyes he deserved it. She had betrayed him, of course. She had been too frightened, too lacking in trust, to go with him."

"What happened to her?" questioned Eleanor gently.

"She died about six years ago," he answered.

"And the young man?"

"Oh, he sold out from the army when his brother died and he came into the title. Since then? Well, I have no doubt that numerous ladies have warned you that I am a rake, a gamester without heart."

She nodded. "They have told me all that, sir, but I find it difficult to believe. You have been kind to me."

"Surely my story has told you why. Why I am *kind*, as you call it. You loved Lennox and to you neither family nor fortune mattered beside that. If only Marianne had had one half of your courage!"

"Perhaps you would not have loved her so much if she had," Eleanor told him softly. "Did you not love her because she was soft and gentle? You wanted to protect her."

He seemed struck by this. "You think I was wrong to expect her to be steadfast?"

"It was not in her nature, Merriot. But perhaps we are both wrong. Perhaps she was simply more virtuous than I. That would be the opinion of the world, you know."

He shrugged. "Perhaps. I do not know anymore. Everything that you have been told about me is true. You must not think that I am any better or more noble than I really am. I have seduced and left many women. Oh, I am not a complete fool. I know that there are many virtuous, admirable women in the world, but I have not sought them. I preferred to spend my time with women whom I despised. It seemed safer, I suppose."

Before she could stop herself, she demanded, "Do you despise Amanda?"

He drew his horses to a standstill once more. He turned to look at her and tried unsuccessfully to take her hand. She withdrew it but with a look in her eyes that told him that it was not dislike of him that made her do so.

"Eleanor, believe me, it is completely at an end between Amanda and myself. But in answer to your question. No, I do not despise Amanda, for she, too, has a kind of courage. She does as she chooses without reference to anyone. She takes her pleasure where she can find it with a lustiness that I cannot but admire. She is not a good woman but at least she is no hypocrite."

Eleanor was glad that he had answered her thus for she was not one of those women who delights in hearing members of her own sex abused. She could not bear to think of his making love to a woman he cared nothing for. It seemed so sad and lonely.

"You do believe me, do you not, Eleanor? Amanda is no longer my mistress. I knew when I saw you last night that I could not go on with it."

He seemed on the point of making some kind of declaration. Hurriedly, she intervened. "Do you not think we should be getting on, Merriot? We shall never get there at this rate!"

He accepted this with a wry smile and for the rest of the outing he kept her amused with his conversation. He was careful, however, to introduce no intimate topics. Nor did he use her name, but returned to the formality of "Miss Portland." When they finally reached the gallery it proved to be well worth a visit, set as it was in the prettiest country, just outside the charming village of Dulwich.

It was late afternoon by the time the carriage drew up once more in South Audley Street. Suddenly it occurred to Eleanor that she had quite forgotten to ask him about Lucy. She had been unforgivably selfish.

"Lord Merriot, will you not come into the house for a moment? There is something I wish to ask of you."

"Naturally, anything in my power," he answered gallantly, but a trifle warily.

She laughed. "Do not worry, my lord. It is nothing disagreeable."

"Oh, well, in that case," he said with a grin and followed her into the house.

"Fiskin, will you please bring tea into the library," she said, as she passed the butler in the hallway. "And send Lucy to me."

Lord Merriot raised his eyebrows. "Lucy?" he repeated.

"Yes, I am sure you remember, my lord. Lucy is the maidservant who has had the misfortune to become . . . that is she . . . you know what I mean?"

"Of course. Can it be that I am to be privileged to assist this Lucy?" he asked quizzically.

She looked at him a little ruefully. "Would you mind very much?" she asked cajolingly.

"On the contrary, I am delighted and profoundly relieved," he answered, smiling at her in a way that brought the blood into her cheeks.

"But why should you be relieved because I ask you to help Lucy?" she demanded, puzzled.

"Why, because I was beginning to think that you had no faults at all. Now I find that you do."

Her eyes were dancing now. "And what, sir, pray tell, are my faults?"

"Why, you are a damned managing woman, my dear," he replied lightly. "I can only hope that you will shortly turn your energies to managing me!"

It was said so humorously that she could not believe he meant her to take him seriously. And if he did his meaning was still in doubt. He had not mentioned marriage at all. Could he really think she would replace Amanda in his life? She was shocked to find that the prospect was not as repugnant as it ought to have been. She took refuge in discussing Lucy.

Merriot had no objection to giving the girl a home. He suggested that his estate in the Lakes was sufficiently far from London to insure that no hint of the baby's real paternity would reach there. Lucy would be introduced as the widow of Merriot's former batman, now unhappily deceased. No one would be surprised at his giving the girl a home under such circumstances. They passed the time before Lucy made her appearance in discussing the beauties of the Lake District of which Eleanor had heard much but which she had never seen.

Lucy, when she at last appeared, was looking a great deal prettier and more composed than when Merriot had last seen her. He thought privately that it would not be very long before she was able to provide her infant with a suitable father. He could think of several young men on the estate who would be only too happy to offer her the protection of their name. The young woman herself was torn between delight in being able to return to the country and desolation at the prospect of being obliged to leave Eleanor.

"I shall miss you, too, Lucy," Eleanor told her kindly. "But this is much the best way for you. You would not be comfortable here."

"How am I to get up there, miss?" asked the girl hesitantly. "It's a right long way I'm thinkin'." It was obvious that she was reluctant to make the journey alone, but Merriot's altruism had its limits. He had no intention of leaving London at this juncture simply to conduct a maidservant to her new post.

Eleanor was for once quite at a loss when fortunately the problem was solved by the unexpected arrival of Lord Portland.

If that gentleman was surprised to discover his sister cosily taking tea with the most notorious rake in town he gave no sign of it, merely shaking hands with Merriot and asking Eleanor to hand him a cup.

Lucy's predicament was explained to him and, much to Eleanor's surprise, he was able to offer a solution. "Well, my dear, I have to go up to Yorkshire myself tomorrow. I was going to tell you this evening."

"There is nothing wrong at home, is there?" exclaimed Eleanor. "Maria is no worse?"

"No, no, nothing like that," his lordship assured her. "Just some tiresome business that I have to attend to personally. Anyhow, I can take the girl with me as far as York and then we can put her on the coach to Keswick. How will that do? I'll send a groom with her the rest of the way if you like."

Eleanor could have embraced her kind-hearted brother. "My dear, dear Peter, that will be perfect. Lucy, I know that you are grateful to his lordship."

"Oh, yes, miss." Lucy curtsied, dimpling prettily at her master. "It is right kind of you, sir. Indeed it is!"

Lord Portland, who did not like to be thanked, brushed aside these unwelcome compliments with an embarrassed grunt.

"No need to thank me. Glad to do what I can. Tell me, Merriot, what do you think of the bill Prinny's pushing for? Do you think it stands a chance of getting through the House?"

The gentlemen began to discuss politics. Eleanor, realizing that neither would take any further interest in the mundane arrangements necessary, departed with Lucy in order to begin the preparations.

She dispatched Lucy to the servants' quarters while she proceded to her bedchamber to look for some old gowns that might reasonably be converted to the little maidservant's use. As she passed Emily's chamber, however, she heard a sound that halted her in her tracks. Inside the room Emily was sobbing as though her heart would break.

chapter 8

Although Eleanor had always been used to comfort the child-ish griefs of her little niece, she was now reluctant to go to her. She knew very well why Emily was sobbing her heart out and the consciousness of her own part in the child's unhappiness threatened to overpower her. She almost passed by, but then, ashamed of her cowardice, she forced herself to tap lightly upon the door and in answer to a fresh burst of wailing she entered the sunny room.

Emily was lying curled up on the bed, her head buried in the soft feather pillow. Her plump shoulders heaved with emotion as the sound of racking sobs emerged, rather muffled, from the bed. In her hand she clutched a crumpled letter which, as her aunt approached, she raised herself enough to fling across the room at her.

"Look! Look at this!" she cried. "See how you have ruined my life!"

"Emily . . . my dear . . . !"

"Oh, do not talk to me! Why could you not have considered me when you disgraced the family so! You should have known how it would be. My heart is broken! I shall never, never love anyone as I love Simon!"

Eleanor made no attempt to defend herself, but instead sat down rather shakily to peruse Simon's simple missive. It stated baldly that his father refused to permit their marriage due to some objection to the family. As Simon had no idea what this objection could be, he concluded that there was some disgraceful secret in which his Emily was involved. Nevertheless, he still loved her and begged her only to wait until he attained his majority when he would be free to claim her.

Eleanor breathed a sigh of relief. "Come now, Emily. This is not so very bad. Simon still loves you. It cannot be so long now before he is one-and-twenty and then you may be happy. I had feared that he had broken with you completely. This is better than I could have hoped."

"I cannot wait a whole six months!" wailed Emily. "You do not understand how I feel. He will have forgotten me by then. I know he will!"

"In that event, Emily, his love will have been worth very little. But I think better of your Simon than you do. He will be true, I am sure of it!"

Emily was in no mood to be pacified. "Yes, but if it were not for you I could be married at once. If you had not run away like that! That must be the reason his father objects to the match, for there is nothing else he can dislike in it!"

Miss Portland laughed rather bitterly. "Oh, yes, you are quite right. Lennox would let you marry Simon tomorrow if it were not for me!"

"I knew it!" exclaimed Emily, and burst into fresh tears.

"But not for quite the reasons that you imagine. Viscount Lennox will not permit Simon to marry you for then he would be obliged to face me."

"Face you, Aunt? What do you mean?" demanded Emily, surprised out of her tantrum.

Eleanor sighed. "It seems to me that I spend half my life discussing this rather stupid episode. It was, after all, only one short night, but I am never to be allowed to forget it for a moment. Well, it is a day for confessions. You see, Emily, Simon's virtuous father is the man with whom I eloped. That is why he does not want his son to marry into this family. He feels, and who can blame him, that it might be a touch embarrassing for him."

"You and Simon's father!" repeated Emily in a shocked whisper. "But we thought it was Lord Merriot!"

Eleanor was startled. "Good heavens, child, whatever put that into your head?"

"It was Harriet's idea. She said that she was sure you were in love with him. You are, aren't you, Aunt Eleanor?"

"You are both very silly children," replied Eleanor, coloring. "Lord Merriot has been kind, but that is all. Anything else is absurd!"

"I do not see why." Emily pouted, her own troubles temporarily forgotten. "I am sure that he is in love with you and not that dreadful Lady Montclair."

"That is enough, Emily. We were discussing your affairs," announced Eleanor hurriedly. "Now I think that you should write to Simon and tell him that you quite understand and are willing to wait to have your engagement announced. Six months will pass by very quickly, I promise you."

Emily heaved a sigh. "I suppose so. Fancy you and Viscount Lennox being in love. Why, he is quite old. I did not think he was romantic enough to do anything like that."

"He is not more than five-and-forty," answered Eleanor, a little piqued.

"Well, that is old," pointed out Emily unanswerably.

"This conversation is quite improper," said Eleanor decidedly. "Write to Simon, my dear. You have my permission to tell him why his father is so against the match. I do not see why he should not know!"

Emily needed no further urging and was able to dry her eyes and settle down quite happily to her task. Six months was after all not so very long and she would have plenty of time to prepare her trousseau.

Simon's joy at receiving this proof of his Emily's exquisite faith in him may be imagined. As for the rest of her communication, he quite rightly considered that it had nothing to do with him and no more affected him than to render him a little indignant toward the father who had sought to blight his prospects for so trivial a cause.

It was in the weeks that followed that Eleanor really began to enjoy herself as she had not in years. She no longer feared the censure of Society for, despite Lady Sefton's grim warnings, the *ton* had apparently decided to accept her back into their exclusive ranks. She was invited everywhere and although her niece and Harriet were included in the invitations, it was Eleanor who shone at these gatherings. Society quickly discovered that she was not only very beautiful. She also possessed a quick wit and a great deal of learning. Eleanor had not allowed the ten years of her exile to pass in barren domesticity. She had read every new work that the York bookshops could furnish. She had keenly followed the politics of the day and was a good deal better informed upon the progress of the war than most of the gentlemen she encountered.

She had unfortunately imbibed a lot of rather radical notions from her reading, upon the rights of man and universal suffrage, but this was held by most people to add to her fascination. In short, Eleanor had in some mysterious way contrived to become the fashion, and being a very human woman she was not above enjoying every minute of it.

As she grew more confident in her powers, she took to holding select little soirées of her own. It was not necessary to be wealthy or well born to be invited to one of these but no one was admitted who had not something fresh, original, or amusing to contribute. Thus on Thursday evenings it was possible to meet at the elegant house in South Audley Street not only such distinguished personages as Mr. Southey and Madame D'Arblay but also writers, clergymen and rising young political figures.

Lord Portland was still out of town, but Eleanor had no fears that he would disapprove of her parties. She never invited anyone whose reputation was in the smallest doubt and was wont to remark ruefully that she was herself the most disreputable person present.

Even more popular than these intellectual gatherings were the informal family parties which she occasionally held on Sunday afternoons. All of Emily's and Harriet's friends would be invited and many hilarious hours would be spent in playing Speculation, Charades, and in small impromptu dances. The girls were in high fettle, for Harriet was growing prettier every day in the consciousness that very soon she would be asked to become Lady Montgomery, while Emily bloomed equally under Simon's tender, if discreet, courtship. They saw each other as much as ever under Eleanor's watchful eye and so did not suffer too much from the enforced secrecy of their betrothal.

Perhaps the only person to view Eleanor's sudden rise to popularity with disapprobation was Lord Merriot. He had rather enjoyed his position as Miss Portland's only friend and supporter. He had looked forward to the time when he should be able to protect her from the censure of the world. Now it appeared that she needed no protection, and so far from being her only friend, he now found it difficult to get near her.

Eleanor had acquired several admirers. The most prominent of these was Mr. Osborne. Merriot did not make the mistake of dismissing this gentleman on the score of his mature years. He was not above fifty and, in his lordship's opinion, dangerously attractive. He knew that Eleanor was not insensible to this and found Mr. Osborne excessively comfortable to talk with. Nor was she wholly indifferent to a very different gentleman, one Reverend Donahue, a fiery Irishman whose work among the poor of London could not but command admiration.

These worthy gentlemen caused Merriot only moderate concern; however, it was a different matter when, arriving at one of Eleanor's Sunday-afternoon gatherings, he found her deep in conversation with a dramatically handsome gentleman whom he had no difficulty in recognizing as the poet Lord Byron who had taken London by storm. The young people were making a great deal of noise and so he could not discover what it was that held Eleanor in such fascinated conversation, but he could not help thinking that the poet's burning eyes might have something to do with her obvious interest.

She glanced up as he approached and gave him a welcoming smile. "Lord Merriot, how kind of you to come and join our silly games. Will you play at Speculation or shall we have Charades instead?"

He smiled, acknowledging a hit. His reluctance to enter into the spirit of these entertainments had more than once been the subject of Eleanor's wit.

"Thank you, ma'am, I had hoped merely to have the pleasure of a little conversation with you," he answered, bowing formally to her companion.

Lord Byron took the hint and rose gracefully. "I have already monopolized you for too long, Miss Portland. Unlike Lord Merriot, I am very fond of Charades and I hope the young ladies will permit me to join them."

Eleanor smiled upon him, reflecting that nowhere did the young poet so forget his affectations as in her drawing room. She thought it must be a relief to him. Merriot, however, caught that tender smile and quite suddenly the jealousy that he had held in check until now consumed him.

"What is that fellow doing here with you?" he demanded in a low tone.

"What do you mean, my lord? Is there any reason why Lord Byron should not be here?" she asked with raised eyebrows.

"Damn it, the man is a popinjay!" responded Merriot, losing his temper as he watched Byron prepare himself for the charade by draping rich shawls around himself like some Indian potentate.

Eleanor laughed. "Why, he is a little vain, I grant you, but such a genius that one must permit his foibles. I find him very conversable."

"That I can see for myself," he answered.

Eleanor began to be a little annoyed. "I do not understand why you should take this tone with me, my lord. Did you come here simply to be disagreeable?"

He was by this time thoroughly enraged and spoke unwisely. "I cannot stand by and watch you behave in this way. You may be indifferent to the conventions if you like, but to encourage the attentions of that flaunting peacock, whom all the world knows to be Caro Lamb's lover, is the outside of enough!"

She answered him icily. "It may interest you to know, my lord, that very much the same words were used to me regarding yourself. If I did not then pay any attention to such warnings, pray why should I do so now? The young man has never treated me with anything but the greatest respect. I wish I could say as much for you!"

By this time the quarrel had reached such proportions that they could not continue with the young people in the room. Eleanor arose in some dudgeon and, charging another lady to keep an eye on the boisterous party, she left. Merriot followed quickly and found her waiting for him in the library.

"Well, Merriot, I would be glad if you would explain why you are behaving in this ridiculous way," she said as soon as he entered. Any thoughts he might have had of apologizing were naturally dismissed by this greeting and he answered her forthrightly.

"I do not wish to see you make a fool of yourself, that is all. The boy is years younger than you."

"Make a fool of myself?" she repeated incredulously. "Is it possible you believe that I would . . . that I am in love with that silly young man? You are insufferable! And he is not years younger than I!"

"Really? Then perhaps I am wrong, perhaps you regard him as an eligible parti. I am sorry to disillusion you, my dear. The title is quite valueless," he told her sarcastically.

"Oh!" gasped Eleanor. "Oh, I should like to hit you for that. What, may I ask, gives you the right to talk to me in this way? What right have you to censure my conduct?"

In answer, Merriot, who was thrown off his stride by the turn of events, made the mistake of striding across the room and jerking her roughly into his arms. "Eleanor, Eleanor!" he muttered huskily and crushed her mouth under his. How she might have responded to this treatment is uncertain for most unfortunately at that moment the door opened and before they could spring apart, Fiskin entered the room.

The butler affected to have seen nothing and conveyed his message to his mistress in the most normal manner, but Eleanor was seriously annoyed to have been placed in such a position and would dearly have liked to slap Merriot's handsome face. However, she contented herself with sweeping him a regal curtsey before bidding him a cold good-bye. Merriot was left feeling rather foolish and not a little angry with himself. However, pleasanter thoughts soon obtruded. It had been every bit as delightful as he had hoped it would be to hold Miss Portland's slender form in his arms. He only hoped that the next time she might be induced to cooperate a little more.

Eleanor, having dealt with the trifling domestic upset requiring her attention, was about to return to the drawing room when she heard the sounds of soft voices from the small salon adjoining it. Conscious that it was her disagreeable duty to investigate, she rapped smartly upon the door and entered the apartment in time to see Harriet and Lord Montgomery in very much the same situation as Fiskin had found herself and Lord Merriot. Harriet, however, showed no disposition to slap his lordship nor did the couple spring guiltily apart. Instead they turned glowing faces to the door, and Harriet cried in a voice of great happiness, "Oh, dear Miss Portland, you will be the first to know. Frederick has asked me to be his wife and I have accepted him!"

"My dear!" exclaimed Eleanor, holding out her arms. "I am enchanted for both of you and I wish you very, very happy."

Lord Montgomery had turned quite red but he watched

Harriet's every move with a sort of doglike devotion and in his eyes Eleanor could read his pride in her. She had always thought him a rather ineffectual young man but his love for Harriet was strong and she thought that this marriage might well be the making of him. She offered him her felicitations with sincere warmth.

"But tell me, my lord. Have you obtained Mr. Milton's consent to this engagement?" she said, still mindful of her responsibilities.

"Oh, yes, that's all right and tight. I wrote to the old gentleman a se'nnight ago and he sent his consent right away. Well, I knew he would because by father wrote to him about settlements and all that. I think my father is pleased to see me settling down. Anyway, he told me that I had shown more sense in picking a wife than he had ever expected."

"What a charming compliment to you, Harriet, my love," remarked Eleanor with a laugh.

Harriet giggled. "I think Frederick's family are quite delightful and I shall love them very much, I know. The announcement is to be made quite soon, so may we go in and tell everyone now, Miss Portland? I am so happy that I want them all to know it!"

"Of course. Shall I do it for you?" asked Eleanor, seeing the familiar red creep back into his lordship's downy cheek.

"I say, ma'am, that would be awfully good of you," he said gratefully.

"I will be most happy. Come, let us return to the drawing room. It is quite shocking that I have been away from my guests for so long. I am ashamed of myself."

Charades were still in progress when the little party returned. Eleanor noticed with a sinking heart that Simon was looking very sulky as Emily was engaged in a striking tableau with Lord Byron which seemed to represent a sultan engaged in purchasing a new member for his harem. Emily made a very appealing picture as she stood as though terrified, her clasped hands raised, imploring the sultan's mercy. Eleanor could hardly blame Simon for resenting the fact that all this loveliness was being displayed primarily for the poet and not for himself.

A swift glance around the room told her that Merriot had departed and she was conscious of a swift stab of disappointment. The man was impossible, but she was sorry that they had parted so angrily. It is not difficult for a woman to forgive a man for losing his head just a little over her charms. Indeed she would find it a great deal harder to forgive him if he did not.

Several of the company glanced up as Eleanor and the happy pair entered the room. It did not require Eleanor's elegant little speech to inform them of the news, for Harriet's smiling face was messenger enough.

The two who had previously been enjoying the center of the stage were now ignored as the young people crowded around the betrothed pair. Harriet and her Frederick were much liked and everyone was anxious to offer felicitations. Harriet blushed and smiled and looked, thought Eleanor, quite beautiful in her happiness. She turned away from the sight to look for her niece and was startled to see upon that damsel's countenance an expression of utter mortification. She thought she could understand how Emily must be feeling and moved toward her with some idea of giving comfort.

"My dear," she said in a low voice. "It will not be long now before you too may announce your betrothal. There are only four months until Simon's birthday."

"No!" exclaimed Emily in a passionate undertone. "Do you think that I intend to stand by and watch Harriet . . . Harriet of all people . . . have all the attention, all the parties that ought to be for me? No, I will not!"

"Emily, I am shocked," her aunt told her in a cold voice. "Selfish and spoiled I knew you to be, but I had thought that at heart you were capable of real affection. I see that I was wrong. Perhaps Lennox was more in the right of it than I when he objected to this match. I should not like to see a fine young man like Simon tied to a vain and silly girl!"

Emily was naturally shattered by this speech and fled from the room with a stifled sob. The knowledge that the reproof was merited did very little to alleviate her unhappiness for now she felt that she had forfeited the love of the entire world with the exception of faithful Simon. It was to Simon that she determined to run.

Quietly she crept out onto the landing and leaned over the balustrade. The guests had not yet started to leave. She ran lightly down the stairs and concealed herself in a convenient alcove, utilized by the footmen to slumber unobserved. There she was able to watch as her aunt's guests took their leave. Soon Simon's beloved form appeared. Her aunt accompanied him but fortunately her name was called by someone in the drawing room and with a graceful curtsey to Mr. Trafford she hurried back.

"Simon," hissed Emily softly. "Simon, over here."

He glanced around bewildered. "Emily, is that you? I've been looking for you for the last half hour. Where have you been?"

"Shsh! Do you want everyone to hear? Simon, come here, I must speak with you."

With a quick glance over his shoulder he joined her in the darkened alcove but his sense of propriety was offended.

"I say, Emily, this is not at all the thing, you know!"

"Oh, Simon, do not be stuffy when I am so unhappy," begged Emily on a sob.

"My love, what is it?" demanded Mr. Trafford, mystified.

She cast herself into his arms and buried her face in the hollow of his shoulder. "Simon, darling, do you not love me?" she asked in a muffled voice.

His arms tightened about her plump shoulders. "Of course I do!"

"Then let us be married now. Right away!" she said, raising her huge brown eyes to his.

"But, Emily, how can we? You know my father has refused his consent."

"Then let us be married without it," said Emily triumphantly. "Let us elope!"

Simon was taken aback but he told himself that his little Emily was too innocent to understand all the implications of what she had said.

"Emily, you know how improper that would be. Why, we should have to fly to the border, and believe me, you would not like it at all. Dashed uncomfortable, for one thing, for we could not stay at posting inns. That's the first place they would look for us. And you would not be able to take your maid or have anyone to look after you."

"I would have you," she answered, standing on tiptoe to kiss the end of his nose.

"Yes, but that is just the problem," he answered testily. "We should be obliged to be together overnight without a chaperone. Your reputation would be completely ruined."

She pouted. "Well, Aunt Eleanor's reputation is gone too and she seems to enjoy herself well enough!"

He sighed. "Emily, there is no use discussing this. It is out of the question."

Twenty minutes later, Emily was engaged in planning the details of their escape while the hapless Mr. Trafford attempted to restrain her more daring flights of fancy.

"Dash it, Emily, I don't see any reason why you should have to dress up as a boy. Besides, nothing I've got would fit you. And I don't think we should go abroad either. Setting aside the fact that there is a war going on, we might not be able to find anyone to marry us for weeks!"

"Well, it would be wonderfully romantic, but I can see that it would not be a very good idea. Very well, then, it must be Gretna Green."

Simon made one last effort. "Are you sure you know what you are doing, Emily? There'll be the devil of a row, you know!"

Tears began to roll down her cheeks and the petal-soft lips trembled. "Simon, if you truly loved me you would not talk like that. Don't you want me?"

He looked down into her flowerlike face and his arms tightened involuntarily. "Oh, yes, sweetheart," he murmured, his lips against hers. "Oh, yes I do."

As her lips parted softly under his he dimly realized that he was irrevocably committed to a course of action that seemed to him fraught with danger and possibly considerable embarrassment as well.

chapter 9

Somewhat to Miss Portland's surprise, Emily appeared the next morning in the sunniest of moods. She seemed to have no recollection of Eleanor's harsh words, but kissed her with all her usual affection. Eleanor was relieved to see that she greeted Harriet even more warmly.

"Oh, Harry, I could not be more pleased by your engagement. I feel partly responsible since Montgomery is Simon's best friend. Really, it is all due to me that you met at all!"

Harriet nodded vigorously. "Indeed it is, and for that reason I want you to be my chief bridesmaid, Emily. You will, will you not? You know we always planned that whichever of us married first would have the other as her bridesmaid."

Emily wished that she could reply that it would be out of her power as by that time she would be a married lady herself. As it was, she accepted with becoming pleasure.

"Of course, Harry. I should love to. What shall you wear?"

The young ladies embarked upon a long and fascinating discussion of the current modes, occasionally appealing to Eleanor for her opinion. Miss Portland attended with only half an ear, however. She was conscious of a little depression that morning and several times caught herself straining to hear the sound of the front door bell. She was annoyed with herself. Merriot was not obliged to visit her and it was ridiculous to sit there waiting for him. Nevertheless, when the bell did eventually ring, she jumped up from her seat and was engaged in smoothing her shining ringlets when Fiskin entered to inform her that the Countess of Radcliff awaited her in the drawing room.

Harriet jumped up, clapping her hands in excitement. "Why, it is Frederick's mama!" she exclaimed. "I had no idea that she intended to wait upon you!"

"It is very polite of her to do so," answered Eleanor calmly. "However, as I am in some respects your guardian at the moment, it is right that she should pay us this visit."

She smoothed her lilac muslin and entered the drawing room with some slight feeling of nervousness. From what Frederick had let fall, she felt that Lady Radcliff must be rather a formidable character. Nothing had prepared her for the lady who now awaited her. She was surprisingly young and still a very beautiful woman.

Eleanor smiled upon her visitor, but was rewarded with no answering warmth. Indeed her ladyship drew back visibly as though in fear of some contaminating contact.

"It is kind of you to call on me, Countess," said Eleanor politely. "Will you not take a seat?"

"Thank you, ma'am, but I prefer to stand," answered her ladyship haughtily.

Eleanor was at a loss but feeling that her guest's odd behavior was no excuse for bad manners in herself, she also remained standing so that the two women were able to survey each other very thoroughly.

"You must be wondering why I have come here," finally remarked the Countess.

"I confess, I am a little puzzled, ma'am," responded Eleanor.

"This is by no means an easy errand, Miss Portland. We have not met before for the path of a woman such as yourself would not ordinarily cross mine but in this case . . ."

Eleanor interrupted swiftly. "May I ask what your ladyship means by *a woman such as myself?*"

"I am sure you comprehend me very well, ma'am," answered Lady Radcliff.

"On the contrary, your ladyship, I should like you to explain yourself!"

"Very well, since you force me to it! You, Miss Portland, are a woman who has disgraced not only herself but her whole sex by behavior so bad that I do not know how to express my disgust. Not content with becoming the mistress of my brother Lennox . . ."

"Your brother!" cried Eleanor.

"Certainly. Were you not aware of the relationship?"

"No, I was not. Frederick never mentioned that he and Simon are cousins."

"They are not. Frederick is the offspring of my husband's first wife. She died."

"I see. But that still does not explain why you have come here today. Did you wish simply to insult me or is there some other reason?"

"May I remind you that you interrupted me as I was about to state the reason for this visit which is, I assure you, every bit as unpleasant for me as it is for you."

"I doubt that, but by all means continue," said Eleanor, seating herself with a weary air.

"As I have said, not only were you my brother's mistress and the cause of great unhappiness at that time, but now you have made yourself the talk of the town with . . . with . . . Merriot. You must see that it is impossible to allow my son's future wife to remain under this roof. Your presence alone could be tolerated, but the continued visits of that man . . . Well, I am sure you understand me."

"Certainly I understand you, Countess. It is your opinion that not only is Merriot my lover, but that I flaunt the relationship in front of the innocent girls in my charge. No wonder that you wish to remove Harriet from the influence of such an abandoned creature as you believe me to be. I am used to such impertinences and I will neither protest my innocence nor argue the matter further. Just tell me what it is that you wish me to do."

The countess gave a wintry smile. "I am relieved to find you so reasonable, Miss Portland. I wish to take Harriet away with me to remain under the protection of my roof until the marriage can take place."

Eleanor gazed at her visitor in amazement. "Is that all? But why could you not simply have invited Harriet to stay? You must have known that she would accept with alacrity. Why was all this necessary?"

The Countess bit her lip. "I do not wish to discuss it with you. Suffice it to say that I have wanted to let you know my opinion of you for a long time. Of course I realize that I am unfashionable. You are queening it over us all now, are you not? They say that even Byron is in your toils. Caro Lamb is wild with jealousy since he started coming to your house. Why men flock to the house of a woman like you is a mystery to me. You should triumph for you have certainly collected a circle of the most dissolute gentlemen in the country!"

Eleanor sprang to her feet and would have answered hotly had not she heard a familiar voice outside the doorway.

"No, do not announce me, Fiskin," she heard him say, pushing open the door. "I think I am expected."

She did not know whether to be glad or sorry. His very presence lent color to the accusations against her yet never had she needed his support more. She almost ran to his side, holding out her hands to him like a child seeking comfort. He caught them in his own.

"L . . . Lord Merriot. I . . . I am so glad that you called," she stammered.

"Merriot!" came the Countess's voice, throbbing with some emotion which certainly was not disgust.

He seemed startled. "Belinda! I beg your pardon . . . Countess. I did not . . . that is, I was not aware that you were acquainted with Miss Portland!"

Eleanor stared at the haughty beauty in amazement. She seemed to have lost all her poise, she was flushed and her blue eyes seemed to swim with unshed tears.

"Merriot," she said again very softly. It was obvious that she had quite forgotten Eleanor's presence. Eleanor pulled her hand from Merriot's and, unheeded, she slipped quietly from the room. She did not, however, escape before hearing the Countess saying in tearful accents: "Robert . . . it has been so long. Why have you been avoiding me?"

Eleanor leaned back against the wainscoting in the hallway, for she felt that her legs might not support her. She felt rather sick as though she had received a physical blow. It seemed they were right who had warned her against this man. First Amanda, now the Countess, and how many others? It was all very well to say that he had changed. How could she be sure that he had not said the same thing to every one of his other conquests. There had been times when she could have staked her life that he loved her and her alone, but from the sound of it the Countess had also staked a good deal, and had lost.

Eleanor was well aware that the dignified thing to do under the circumstances was to retire to her room until both Merriot and the Countess had left the house. This course of action did not recommend itself to her, however. She was furiously angry and intended to have the satisfaction of making Merriot every bit as uncomfortable as she was herself. As for the Countess, it seemed that she was miserable enough already. Now Eleanor could understand why the woman had come to see her. "How she must hate me," she thought. "First her brother and now Merriot. I suppose she wanted to take a look at the woman who had taken so much from her. Well, if it is any satisfaction to her, I had little enough joy from either of them!"

She heard the door close and the sweep of the Countess's silks as she departed. She stood for a moment collecting herself and then, straightening her shoulders, she stalked into the drawing room, prepared to fight.

Merriot was standing by the window, and angry though she was, her heart betrayed her at the sight of his manly figure silhouetted against the bright sunshine. The light dazzled her eyes a little so that she could not read the expression in his eyes, but his voice, when he spoke, was gentle, almost tender.

"Eleanor, my dear, it seems that I must always be apologizing to you. I had come to beg your forgiveness for my absurd behavior yesterday. Now I find that because of me you have had a most unpleasant interview. What can I say other than that I am truly sorry?"

She felt her sustaining anger slipping away from her and in its place tears stung her eyes. She sank wearily into a chair.

"It is of no use, Merriot. I have borne enough. I cannot go on like this," she told him, her head in her hands.

He crossed the room swiftly and laid his hand upon her shoulder. She shrugged him off furiously. "Oh, why did you come here? Why did you not leave me in peace? I was contented enough until I met you. Now you have taught me to care for you but there is nothing but misery for me in this! Will you leave me now as you left all the others? Or no, I suppose you have not finished with me yet. I have not given you the supreme conquest you desire. Well, I will inform you, sir, that I have no intention of becoming yet another of your discarded mistresses. Now I wish that you will go away!" she finished pettishly.

"Is that really what you want?" he asked in a quiet tone.

In answer, the self-contained Eleanor burst into tears and he could get no further word from her.

Irrationally, although everything she said of him was the truth, Merriot was cut to the quick by her accusations. The emotion he felt for Eleanor was so unlike anything he had experienced in his other love affairs that he could not understand why she did not immediately sense that this was different. In the beginning certainly, he had intended to seduce her if he could, but that motive had for so long now been superseded by a more noble desire to protect and cherish her that he had forgotten it himself.

"Eleanor, my darling, please do not weep like this. You will make yourself ill. Believe me, there is nothing between Belinda and myself any longer. It was years ago!"

She raised her head at that. "What, was she before Amanda, then? Or was there some other lady between them? I congratulate you, sir! You seem to be most fortunate with my sex. Or is it simply that you never dispatch one mistress until you are sure of the next? I must be a sad disappointment to you. You should not have been so quick to break with Amanda. Well, I daresay she will have you back!"

He looked as though he would have struck her. "By God, ma'am, I have accepted much abuse from you, but this is outside enough! I have no intention of returning to Amanda nor to any other of my *conquests*. But do not imagine that I shall continue to importune you. Obviously my presense is distasteful to you and I shall presently relieve you of it. First, however, there is something I wish to say to you."

"Well, my lord?" she said, her dignity somewhat impaired by a sniff.

"It is simply this. I believed I had found in you a woman whom I could love, not as a plaything but as a wife in whom I could confide as an equal, a mother for my sons. I have admitted that my life until I met you will bear little scrutiny. I thought that you understood. But if my present affection has not the power to overcome your aversion to my former way of life then I will leave you, ma'am. Please accept my wishes for your future happiness."

She lifted her head, but was too choked with tears to speak. He turned in the doorway and studied her for a few moments as though wishing to impress her image upon his memory. "God bless you, my love," he said softly, and left.

It was hardly surprising that in the days that followed Emily complained that her Aunt Eleanor was no fun at all. She was quite unable to support her spirits under the consciousness that had she not thrown away her chances of happiness she might even now be planning her own wedding rather than merely assisting Harriet in preparing for hers. Even that solace would soon be denied her, however, for Harriet had accepted her future mother-in-law's invitation and was to remain in the house for less than a week before she departed.

The two girls often discussed Eleanor for her unhappiness was obvious and they had not been blind to the fact that Lord Merriot no longer visited.

"Do you suppose they have quarreled?" asked Harriet, as they sat sorting ribbons in her pretty bedchamber.

"I should think it must have been very serious if they did. She does not watch for the post or listen for the doorbell anymore. She would if she thought there was any chance of seeing him again," responded Emily shrewdly.

"Well, I think it is a terrible shame. I wish there was something we could do," sighed Harriet. "I hate to see poor Miss Portland so unhappy!"

"Oh, well, there is nothing to be done. Tell me, what are you going to wear for the ball?" asked Emily. The dance in question was to be held in Harriet's honor by the Countess of Radcliff and it promised to be an event of no common splendor. All the world and his wife would be there, including Eleanor, who had confidently expected to be excluded from the guest list. When the invitation did arrive she could hardly be persuaded to accept. Emily finally convinced her that it was impossible for her to attend if Eleanor were not there to chaperone her and, mindful of her duty as always, she agreed. Having done so she could not help wondering whether Merriot would be present. Not that it was of any consequence, of course, but there could be no harm in wearing one's newest ball gown.

There were still several days before the ball and Eleanor had accepted an invitation to dine at Lady Jersey's before going on with her party to Almacks. She had not in the least wished to do so, but her ladyship had roundly informed her that wearing her heart upon her sleeve in this nonsensical manner would give people even more to talk of than she had already given them. This naturally brought up Eleanor's chin in defiance. She could not bear to think of her affairs being discussed by all the fashionables, particularly as their gossip might reach Merriot himself. She would not have it said that she too had gone into a decline on his account!

Almacks held no terrors for Eleanor now. Even the acidic Mrs. Carruthers had unbent enough to favor her with a civil bow in passing, and among the patronesses she knew herself to be a favorite. She had taken considerable pains with her appearance that night and was in great beauty. She wore a ball gown of ivory lace trimmed with seed pearls, cunningly devised so that it fell in graceful folds from the shoulders and caught under the bosom with gold-spangled ribbons. Many ladies exclaimed over this gown and were suitably impressed when Eleanor explained that the idea was quite her own.

Harriet had by this time removed to her betrothed's house and was therefore absent. Emily had pettishly declared that Almacks was the dullest thing and so Eleanor had no duties of chaperonage to perform but was free to enjoy the assembly for its own sake. She did not lack for partners, and despite the fact that Merriot put in no appearance, she found that she was enjoying herself.

Shortly before supper as she sat fanning herself after an energetic waltz, she heard her name spoken softly and looked up to see the gentlemanly form of Mr. Osborne making his way across the crowded room to her side. Eleanor was pleased to see him for of late he had been absent from the Thursday-night salon. She taxed him upon this and he explained readily. "Indeed I regret my absence greatly, ma'am, but the truth is that I have had to go down to the country. My youngest child was sick of the measles and calling for me. Having entered her chamber I had myself to be quarantined until the danger of infecting others was at an end."

"I did not know, sir, that you had any young children. Pray, how old is the little girl?"

"She is but nine years old, Miss Portland. It is a matter of concern to me that she is being brought up in such a scrambling way, but what can a mere father do? My eldest daughter, Louisa, has been a mother to all her brothers and sisters, but she is to be married soon herself. I am at my wits' end!"

Eleanor swallowed. "How many children do you have then, Mr. Osborne?" she asked.

"Twelve in all," he told her proudly.

"What a fine family, sir," she said as he seemed to expect some comment.

He smiled at her warmly. "I am happy that you think so, ma'am, for I have something to say to you upon the subject. Will you permit me to call on you? Tomorrow perhaps?"

Eleanor was at a loss. "Certainly, sir, if you wish, but . . ."

"But?" he prompted.

She hesitated. "Never mind, sir. Certainly I should be happy to receive you."

"May I bring Miss Osborne to be presented to you also? She has heard so much about you and is anxious to make your acquaintance."

She could not but be pleased by such distinguishing attention, but she wished that she could in some way prevent the declaration which seemed imminent. Had she not given her heart to Lord Merriot, she owned to herself that she would have been strongly tempted by Mr. Osborne's offer. He was by no means unattractive, while the prospect of so numerous a family in need of her affection was appealing. She liked Osborne too well, however, to offer him Spanish Coin. He wanted more than just a mother for his children in the lady he married or surely he would have found a wife long before this. She could not give him the love she had a right to expect in his wife, she had only sincere friendship to offer him. She knew from the look in his eyes when they rested upon her that such lukewarm sentiments would not be enough.

She found Miss Osborne to be everything that was most proper and elegant. She had a graceful person, a well-informed mind and, judging from her smiling eyes, a great deal of humor. Eleanor would have liked to make a friend of her. It was a pity that her refusal of the father must necessarily put an end to any chance of friendship with the daughter.

After some half hour had passed in pleasant chat, Miss Osborne announced that she must leave as she was to walk with some friends in the Park. Her father, however, made no move to depart and as soon as his daughter had left the house, he began to speak. Eleanor could not hear him unmoved. He spoke well and with every sentence she became more convinced that this man loved her with a sincere and strong affection.

"Will you not give me your answer, dear Miss Portland? You cannot know how I am tormented by this suspense," he said at last, his eyes fixed upon her delicately flushed face.

She lifted her eyes and no doubt he read her answer there for the eager expectation died out of his own.

"Mr. Osborne. It is customary to answer a proposal by first expressing a sense of the honor done by it. Believe me when I say that these are not empty words. I am honored, far more than I can express, by your affection. I wish with all my heart that it were possible for me to return it. I have for you the very greatest liking and respect, indeed I do, but . . ."

He smiled sadly. "I think I know the reason for that *but*. I am too late, am I not? I feared it but I wish you very happy. I have observed Lord Merriot's attentions to you and I believe that his love for you is as strong as my own. No doubt he will make you very happy."

"You are mistaken, sir. I shall not marry Merriot," she interrupted.

"Why then there is hope for me!" he exclaimed eagerly.

She shook her head. "I could not marry you, sir, knowing that my heart is already given to another man."

He frowned, puzzled. "Is it Donahue, then?"

"Good Lord, no! Mr. Osborne, I owe you the truth, but it is painful to speak of it. You were right in thinking that I am in love with Lord Merriot, but for reasons I cannot discuss, it is impossible that I should marry him. Feeling as I do, I cannot marry anyone else either. So you see I must refuse your proposal, deeply though I regret the unhappiness I must cause you."

His expression lightened. "My dear, I understand and honor your feelings, but what you have said gives me some hope. Perhaps in the future, when you have had a little time to recover from your present unhappiness, you may see my offer in a more favorable light. I shall hope so in any event."

Eleanor was sure that this was unlikely, but she did not see how she could forbid the man to hope and so she said nothing, merely entreating his silence with a gesture.

When he had left, she felt even more lonely and bereft than before. Her resentment against Merriot illogically increased as though he were responsible for the disappointment of a man so good and so deserving of love. Drearily she faced the future and saw before her nothing but a return to Hawthorne Place where once more she would be at the beck and call of her sister-in-law and be obliged to face the Society which had ostracized her. The prospect was almost enough to make her send after Osborne, but her innate sense of right and wrong prevented her. To marry him would be an easy way out of her dilemma but she knew that she had sacrificed her right to an easy or happy life and she would now pay the price for it all the long, lonely years of her life.

chapter 10

Lord Merriot had passed the last few days in a state of uncharacteristic indecision. He was a proud man who, since his early disappointment, had determined to pursue no unwilling woman. Unfortunately, his feelings for Eleanor were stronger than he had known. He was unable to banish her from his thoughts. Their friendship had been brief, composed of nothing more than a few highly charged encounters, yet still her image lingered in his memory as no other woman's had done. He had to see her again, for if ever he were to sleep well at night he must once more hold her in his arms and feel her soft lips trembling beneath his own.

Thus it was that he determined to accept Lady Radcliff's invitation. Normally he avoided the woman for she had been the most difficult of all his mistresses to detach. He remembered scenes that had lasted weeks, notes of impassioned entreaty, veiled visits to his home. He had tried to be gentle but in the end only his palpable indifference had convinced her that all was at an end. Now, his own heart bruised by another, he felt more sympathy for Belinda than he had ever felt before. It was no easy thing, he discovered, to have one's love thrown back in one's face as a thing of no value.

Meanwhile Eleanor also had come to the decision that she must see Merriot once more. No doubt she had killed all his love for her, but she wanted him to know that she had been wrong, that she did understand and forgive his past mistakes, just as he had forgiven hers. Then, she supposed, she would be able to return to Pudsley and live in peace. It was a depressing prospect.

Emily also was unusually nervous that day. She could not sit still but fidgeted around the house until Miss Portland, who was attempting to compose her own mind by reading Mr. Southey's improving work, *The Life of Nelson*, found herself quite unable to concentrate. She suggested instead that they take a walk in the spring sunshine.

It was not the hour of the fashionable promenade, and save for a few other nature lovers, they had the Park to themselves. It was long since they had been entirely alone together as they used to be. They found themselves talking more confidentially as the ease of their former intercourse returned.

Eleanor was able to say something that had been troubling her mind for some time. "I want to tell you how sorry I am that my differences with Viscount Lennox have caused you some distress, my dear. You know that I would have given a great deal to have saved you from this situation. To be entering into a secret engagement at your age is difficult."

Emily smiled sunnily at her aunt. "Oh, do not worry about that, Aunt Eleanor. In a way it is rather romantic to be secretly engaged. It seems more so than Harriet's engagement which I find sadly commonplace."

Eleanor laughed. "Well, that is one way of looking at it, infant. Is Simon proving faithful?"

"Oh, yes! I never really doubted that he would be. Is it not strange how being truly loved by someone as good as he makes you feel unworthy. I cannot understand why a man like Simon should love a silly, frivolous creature like me, but he does!"

"I think that everyone feels the same way, my dear. That is why love comes as such a surprise, particularly if one is lucky enough to be loved by the gentleman of one's choice. It seems almost too good to be true that he should feel the same way, does it not?"

Emily cast her aunt a swift look from under her lashes. "Is

that how you felt when Lord Merriot fell in love with you?" she asked, greatly daring.

Suddenly the need to confide her troubles swept over the competent Miss Portland. She found herself pouring out the whole story to her young niece who nodded wisely as a sage as she listened.

"Do you still care for him, Aunt Eleanor?" she asked as the recital came to an end.

"Of course I do!" responded Eleanor, rather crossly.

Emily's young face assumed a rather stern expression. She looked her aunt firmly in the eye and said, "Then you must get him back!"

"Emily!"

"Oh, don't you see? I love you so much that I cannot bear the thought of your going back to Hawthorne Place to be bullied and talked about by people who cannot appreciate how fine you are. It would be so much better to marry him, even if you were a little unhappy sometimes. Perhaps he might not always be faithful or kind, but at least you would be alive and not buried in that hole of a village. Aunt, don't you see, you have no right not to try!"

Miss Portland was naturally taken aback, much as she would have been had her tortoiseshell kitten suddenly opened its pink mouth to lecture her. "Why, Emily, you have grown up all of a sudden!" she said in wonder.

"Oh, that happened ages ago," Emily assured her, smiling happily. "Now you will try, won't you, Aunt Eleanor?"

Eleanor smiled back. "My dear, what on earth have I got to lose?"

In companionable silence they strolled back to the house. Both ladies had much to think about, not least the consideration of their toilettes for the evening. Therefore they returned to their respective chambers as soon as they entered the house and did not meet again until it was time to set out for Harriet's ball.

Emily hardly recognized her friend that night as they ascended the stairs to be received by the Earl and Countess. Harriet, so splendidly dressed and covered in jewels, seemed completely changed. It was only when she clasped Harriet's hand for a moment and felt how icy cold it was that she realized that her friend was in fact in a state of nervous collapse. She gave her an encouraging grin which won an answering gleam.

"Well, Harry, you are very fine tonight. What emeralds!"

"Oh, yes, are they not beautiful? They are always presented to the heir's betrothed. It's a family tradition. Oh, Emily, what if I should lose some of them?"

"Don't be silly! Why should you?" answered her friend bracingly before she moved on.

Eleanor now moved forward and curtsied to Lady Radcliff who gave her the frostiest of smiles and a slight inclination of the head. Miss Portland was thankful when the meeting was over. She had almost expected to be ordered out of the house.

She was besieged by admirers the moment she appeared in the ballroom and had the greatest difficulty in retaining two dances for his lordship, should he condescend to appear.

The first dance was a quadrille in which she played her part with her usual spirit and elegance. Halfway down the set she suddenly realized that Merriot had arrived and was watching her with rather a grim expression on his face. Her bright smile faded as she saw him turn away to chat animatedly with some lady who had hailed him eagerly. Yet another of his loves, she supposed. Then she scolded herself for such pettiness. Why should he not speak to another lady since she was engaged in the dance? If she were to be as jealous as that she might as well give up all ideas of winning back his affection.

Merriot meanwhile was paying very little heed to his companion's discourse, being more occupied in following every graceful move Miss Portland made. When her partner spoke to her and she answered with an enchanting smile, Merriot ground his teeth.

"I beg your pardon, sir?" said the lady, interrupted in mid-speech.

"Nothing, ma'am, nothing at all. May I beg the honor of leading into the next set?" he answered, turning his back upon the distracting Miss Portland.

"Oh, my goodness, I do not know if I have a dance free!" exclaimed his companion mendaciously. "Ah, yes! As it happens, the next one is unengaged. I should be most happy, sir."

"Good!" answered Merriot shortly.

Eleanor had noticed his dark looks. Had he come merely to glower at her? The man was impossible. Would he ask her to dance? She had saved the supper dance. If only she had a chance to talk to him then she could judge his feelings toward her.

Her partner led her back to her seat as the music ceased but almost immediately the next gentleman came to claim her for the cotillion. She could have wept with vexation for Merriot had seemed on the point of making his way over to her side when the importunate partner arrived. This was nothing, however, to the mortification that swept over her when she saw him lead his partner into her own set. He caught her eye and bowed with frigid politeness.

The half hour of the dance was pure misery for Eleanor. Merriot stood only a few feet from her and, she was aware, listened to every word that passed between herself and her partner. As this gentleman was a notorious flirt, she was in a continual flurry lest some words of his might make Merriot lose what little control he retained over his temper. Yet even as she worried over this possibility she was conscious deep down inside of the first tentative stirrings of happiness. No man surely would behave in this absurd fashion if he were not insanely jealous. He must love her still! She glanced up to find his eyes upon her and all unconsciously she gave him a smile so sweet and loving that he blinked. Then an answering smile crept into his own and he raised his hand in salute.

She returned with renewed animation to the demands of the dance, sure now that he would approach her as soon as the set concluded. Alas, for such plans. No sooner was she seated than yet another gentleman appeared—Mr. Osborne.

"Miss Portland, no words of mine can describe your beauty tonight. You are radiant," he told her in a low voice.

She smiled but her heart sank. Here was one man whom she owed attention. She could not get rid of him in the hope that Merriot would come to her.

"You must allow me to tell you how very much Miss Osborne enjoyed meeting you. She was quite delighted by you as I had known she must be."

"And I with her," answered Eleanor sincerely. "Miss Osborne is a very lovely young lady. You should be proud of her."

"I am honored by your opinion, ma'am. It would give me great pleasure to see the two of you become friends," he answered significantly.

She realized that she had been too open in her admiration and, fearing that he had misinterpreted her, she relapsed into silence.

"May I ask if you are engaged for the supper dance?" he

asked presently. "I should be honored to take you in if you are not."

She knew not how to answer, but was spared the trouble by Lord Merriot who had approached unnoticed and now answered for her. "Your pardon, Osborne, but Miss Portland is promised to me."

"I see. Then I will not stay. I wished you happy before, ma'am, and you assured me that my felicitations were inappropriate. I shall venture to offer them again." With that he kissed her hand and left.

Merriot seated himself beside her. "What did the fellow mean by that?"

Eleanor turned on him. "And what did you mean by saying that I was engaged to you for the supper dance? You know it is not so. I would not have been so rude to Mr. Osborne for the world!"

"I notice that you did not contradict me," he said with a grin.

"Merriot you . . . you . . . !"

"Yes, I know, but we cannot quarrel in comfort here, my darling. Let us retire to a more secluded spot where you have my permission to call me as many names as you can lay your tongue to."

"I cannot go off with you like that. What would people say?" said Eleanor in a sudden panic.

"Eleanor, if you do not come with me, I shall pick you up and carry you, which would, I assure you, cause a great deal more talk!"

She did not believe him, but something in his voice warned her that he would not in this case take no for an answer.

"Oh, very well," she said with a vain assumption of ease. "Although I cannot imagine what it is that you wish to say to me!"

"And that my love is the first untruthful statement I have ever heard from your lips. You know very well what I wish to say to you."

They had reached an arched doorway before which stood a stolid lackey. Merriot said something in a low voice and slipped a gold coin into this worthy's hand. The man nodded, his expression unchanged, and Merriot, taking her by the arm, led her through the door into a small salon lit only by the moonlight streaming in through the long windows.

"What did you say to that man?" she demanded as the door closed behind them.

"I told him to make sure that we were quite undisturbed, my love," he answered, smiling at her in a way that made her suddenly tremble.

"Merriot, I . . ."

"My sweet Eleanor, will you not try to call me Robert. I have an ambition to hear my name upon your lips."

"Robert, then. We should not be here. It will be remarked."

In answer he held out his hand. "Come here, Eleanor," he commanded as though talking to a recalcitrant child.

"Yes, Robert," she said and laid her hand in his.

He drew her gently toward him until she stood so close that he could feel her warmth and smell the scent of violets that clung about her.

"Well, my love, you are here at last," he said tenderly. "My dear and only love, will you trust me now? Will you believe that you are the last woman in my life, that there will never be another? Will you allow me to make you happy?" he asked, his lips against her bright hair.

She raised her head from his shoulder and lifted her face to his like a child asking to be kissed. He stood gazing into her face for a long moment and then with a great sigh he folded her in his arms and bent his head to hers.

"Robert . . . Robert," she sighed, when she could speak.

"Eleanor," he answered, burying his face in the soft nape of her neck.

She lifted a hand to stroke his crisp, dark hair. "I have been very foolish, Robert. I should have trusted you, but I was afraid to let myself love again. Can you understand that?"

He smiled lovingly. "I will try to forgive you if you will say it now. You have not yet, you know."

"Have I not? I thought I must have told you long ago. I love you, Robert, with all my heart. I am yours if you want me for as long as I live."

"If I want you! My God, do you never look at yourself in the mirror? You have no need to be humble, my lovely one."

She offered her lips once more and he responded with gratifying fervor to the invitation.

"However pleasant this is, I think that we should leave," he said presently. "If I am not to ravish you here and now!"

She laughed. "Oh, am I in danger, then?"

"More than you know, my damnably seductive little love!"

"Almost you tempt me to stay," she murmured with a wicked smile.

"Oh, no, my sweet. When I make love to you it will not be upon a sofa with a footman standing guard outside the door," he told her.

"I love you, love you, love you," was her sensible reply.

"We must go!" he said hurriedly and almost thrust her from the room before temptation overcame him.

This little scene was by no means the only *tête-à-tête* taking place that evening. Several ladies and gentlemen, influenced no doubt by the champagne which was served in lavish quantities, had found similar isolated apartments and obliging footmen. Simon and Emily were among them. They had, however, more pressing business than mere dalliance. The sight of Harriet in all her glory had been too much for Emily. She would be put off no longer. They must elope tomorrow.

"But how?" demanded Simon. "How are you going to get away without being seen? Even if your maid did not hear you go there is a footman on duty all night. You could never get out of the house!"

"Yes, but I need not go from the house. I have been thinking and I have an excellent plan. Do but listen!"

Simon, much as he loved her, had little faith in his Emily's ability to organize such an undertaking, but when she had set forth her idea he was obliged to own that it might work.

"It is very simple. You must ask Aunt Eleanor and me to go to Vauxhall tomorrow night. There is to be a masked ball. We have nothing planned and I can persuade her to go with us, I am sure. Then halfway through the evening I shall say that I have the headache and you will offer to take me home . . ."

"Yes, but your aunt won't want to stay at Vauxhall by herself. She will want to come too," objected Simon.

"Not if Harriet and Montgomery are there. She will have to stay to chaperone Harriet. We must confide in them a little for Harry will offer to return with us, if I know her, but I shall tell her that she must insist that she is enjoying herself and wants to stay. Aunt Eleanor will not be so rude as to leave."

"Well, it might work, Emily. I could have a carriage waiting at the entrance. Would not your aunt look in on you when she comes in, though? We should need a night's start if we are not to be stopped halfway to Scotland."

"No, she will not for she knows that sleep is the only cure for my dreadful headaches and she would not risk waking me. Oh, Simon, please let us try!"

He was not proof against the pleading look in her eyes. "Oh, very well, Emily. I'll go find Freddy. We need their help and for all I know they may be engaged elsewhere tomorrow night!"

But as it chanced, the betrothed couple were quite free and enchanted by the notion of visiting the famous gardens.

"I should like it of all things!" exclaimed Harriet. "I do not know how it comes about, but I have not yet seen Vauxhall. Frederick, your mama will have no objection?"

"Not if Miss Portland is to be of the party, I daresay," answered Lord Montgomery good-naturedly. "Let's go and ask her now."

"There is just one thing, Freddy," said Simon in an embarrassed voice. "I can't explain properly, but there is something we want you and Harriet to do for us."

Meanwhile Eleanor was circling happily around the ballroom clasped in Merriot's arms.

"Do you remember the first time we waltzed together?" she asked foolishly.

"How could I forget it? You disliked me intensely and I had never held a more exciting woman in my arms."

"I did not dislike you! I was just afraid and embarrassed," she protested.

His arm tightened about her waist. "I would very much like to kiss you here and now in front of all these very respectable people," he told her.

The music ended but he showed no signs of leaving her side. People were beginning to notice. She saw several ladies with their heads together, but their chatter could not disturb her happiness.

She was so taken up with Merriot that she had quite forgotten that she was supposed to be chaperoning Emily. She had not laid eyes on the child for over an hour but she felt no disposition to go in search of her. In her present humor she merely hoped that she was enjoying herself somewhere in her Simon's arms.

However, the errant couple did eventually appear, full of a scheme to visit Vauxhall the following night.

"Do say you will come, Aunt Eleanor. We should so like

to go. There is to be a masked ball and all manner of entertainments."

Merriot leaned over her shoulder and murmured, "I will meet you there. We will dance together, my love."

She smiled. "Well, if you are all so set on Vauxhall then by all means let us go."

Emily clapped her hands in excitement. "Thank you so much, dearest, kindest Aunt. It will be a wonderful night, I know!"

Eleanor glanced up at Merriot's handsome face. "Yes," she murmured with a tender little smile. "Yes, Emily, I think it will!"

chapter 11

It would be no exaggeration to say that as Lord Merriot made his way through the dark streets that night, he was happier than he had been since the days of his untroubled youth. The consciousness that he had won the love of a woman whom he not only adored but whose intellect he admired and whose character he respected gave him renewed hope of a life composed of those domestic joys which he had renounced years ago as being for other men, not for him. He savored again the sensation of holding her in his arms and the quiet visions of home and children receded before a sudden overwhelming tide of desire. He reflected rather ruefully that if he were to retain his sanity it would be as well if the wedding were not long postponed.

He found that he had arrived in St. James without having the smallest recollection of how he had got there. He let himself in for he did not encourage his servants to wait up for him and was therefore considerably surprised to be met at the door by his valet.

"What the devil's the matter, Weston?" he demanded.

"There was no need for this. You should have been in bed hours ago!"

"So I should have been, my lord, had not the lady arrived just as I was on the point of going up. I thought it best to remain, sir. Not being sure whether you wished to see her ladyship or not."

For one wild moment Merriot had thought the man referred to Eleanor and his heart had begun to beat wildly. Weston's last words disabused him of this pleasant misapprehension.

"Her ladyship?" he repeated on a note of inquiry.

"Lady Amanda, sir. She arrived about an hour ago and insisted on seeing you. When I told her that you were not at home she said that she would wait for you. I beg pardon if I did wrong to allow it, sir, but I knew of no way to stop her ladyship."

"No, no, you could not turn her out, I suppose. I had better see her. Where have you put her?" said Merriot with an abstracted frown.

"In the library, sir. There was still a fire in there. And I should say, sir, that her ladyship asked me to bring her some wine, which I did. She's had pretty near a whole bottle!"

The prospect of facing an angry and possibly inebriated woman at this hour was not one which greatly appealed to him.

"That will be all, Weston. You may go to bed now," he said.

The manservant cast his master a look in which fellow feeling and respect were nicely blended. "Er . . . if you should need me, sir . . . I shall be awake."

"Thank you. You are a good fellow, but I do not anticipate any problems. Good night."

"Good night, sir."

Amanda was found comfortably disposed upon one of my lord's elegant couches, sipping a glass of ruby-colored wine. Her hair was unbound and fell about her bare shoulders like a dark cloud. She smiled languorously at Merriot as unembarrassed as though she were there by his invitation.

"Robert, darling. I thought you would never get here. I have been waiting for you this age," she said in her most seductive voice.

He could not but be stirred by the sight of her in her careful disarray, but the memory of Eleanor was still strong and he said, brusquely enough, "Well, I am here now. What is it that you want, Lady Amanda?"

"Goodness, are we not formal?" she tittered. Suddenly she swung her legs to the floor and held out her hands to him. "Help me up, Robert. I fear I have had a little too much of your excellent wine!"

Reluctantly he took her hands and steadied her as she came to her feet.

"You were always so strong," she whispered. He tried to disengage his hands, but hers clung. "Robert, you must know why I have come here! Robert, I love you and I know you love me. Come back to me, my darling. I promise there will be no others for me if you will!"

He stared at her, puzzled. He had not known that she was capable of such strong feeling as she now displayed. He felt guilty suddenly remembering that he had treated her shabbily, believing that her feelings for him were as shallow as his were for her.

"My dear, I am sorry," he said, very gently.

Her eyes widened in astonishment. She had been very sure of her victory. "But why?" she demanded, quite forgetting to be seductive.

"Because I am about to contract another engagement. I am sorry, Amanda, but I am going to be married."

"Married? You! Oh, you are joking me!" she exclaimed, searching his grave face with her huge eyes.

He shook his head. "No, Amanda. So you see you must go, my dear. I do not wish to distress you, but there is nothing for you here."

Her eyes half closed. "Nothing? There is this!" she answered, and, flinging her arms around his neck, she pressed her ripe mouth to his in a passionate kiss.

It says a great deal for Eleanor's redeeming influence that after a first instinctive response Merriot calmly unclasped the clinging arms and gently put her from him. "It is useless, my dear," he told her. Then recollecting a recent *on dit*, he said, "I had thought you had already found someone to take my place. Is not young Ravenscar a frequent visitor?"

Amanda, angry and frustrated, was betrayed into speaking the truth. "Aye, the boy is a good enough lover, but he has not a feather to fly with and the duns are after me again. Robert,

I am at my wits' end. Where will I get the money if you will not help me?"

His eyes were alight with amusement and relief. "So that is what all this is about. And I was afraid I had broken that tender heart. My dear, why did you not say so in the first place? How much do you want?"

"Robert, do you mean it?" she exclaimed. "I need all of five thousand!"

He was startled. "You have been busy, have you not, Amanda? What was it? Faro?"

"As you say. Well, will you give me the money?" she demanded.

"Since you put it so charmingly, how can I refuse?" he answered mockingly. "Let us call it a parting gift. You understand me? There must be no more scenes like this one!"

"Robert, if you will give me that money I will never come near you again, I promise," she answered eagerly.

He smiled. "There is no need to go that far, Amanda. I am afraid, however, that I do not have that sum in the house. I will have to get it for you tomorrow. Shall you be at home?"

"I have stupid engagements all day. Montclair is home, you know. I will have to meet you somewhere."

"Very well. I shall be at Vauxhall tomorrow evening. I shall see you there. You know the small pavilion by the river gate?" he asked.

Her eyes glinted provocatively. "Of course," she answered with a naughty smile.

"Oh, one of your trysting places, is it?" he smiled. "Very well, ten o'clock in the pavilion. Do not be late."

"I would never keep a man with five thousand guineas waiting," she said with refreshing honesty.

He laughed. "Amanda, you are a jade, but an amusing one. I hope Ravenscar knows how to keep you in line."

"Not as you did, Robert." She eyed him from under her lashes. "Would you like me to show you how very grateful I am?" she asked in a dulcet tone.

Rather hurriedly he flung open the door. "I thank you but no," he answered, holding it for her to pass through.

"What a pity. I would have enjoyed it," she whispered, reaching up one hand to pat his cheek. "Thank you, Robert, for everything!"

As soon as she had departed Merriot strode quickly back

into the library and poured himself a liberal draft of wine. He reflected that a life of virtue was more hazardous than he had previously any idea of. He hoped his new-found virtue would not be tried quite so temptingly again. He was not sure his nerves could stand the strain!

Eleanor awoke the next morning to a day of bright spring sunshine which accorded well with her mood. She surprised her abigail by rising betimes and although she could not see his lordship until the evening she dressed herself in one of her prettiest gowns, a soft primrose sarcenet, as a kind of tribute to the happiness of the day.

She found Emily already at the breakfast table when she entered the morning room, and it was evident that she, too, was in a mood of considerable exaltation. The two women greeted each other with affectionate gaiety and exchanged compliments.

"My dearest Emily, how becomingly you look. I think you grow prettier every day!" exclaimed Eleanor, bestowing a kiss upon her niece's soft pink cheek.

"And you look as though you had just been given the most wonderful present, Aunt Eleanor," responded Emily shrewdly. "I thought that Lord Merriot seemed very attentive last night!"

Eleanor laughed. "Well, my love, why should I not tell you? It was partly your doing, you know. You told me to get him back and I did, only it was he did it all. Oh, I am so happy! He will be at Vauxhall tonight!"

Emily clasped her hands together. "Aunt, how wonderful! Am I to wish you happy?"

Eleanor blushed and nodded. "But do not tell a soul, Emily. I have not written to your father yet, and it would be most improper not to consult him first."

"Oh, I forgot, there is a letter for you from Papa! Here it is."

Eleanor perused the brief note quickly. "Emily, how nice. Your papa will be leaving Pudsley for London tomorrow. He should be here late the following night, he says."

Emily turned a little pale. "Tomorrow!" she exclaimed.

"Yes. Why, what is the matter, my love?"

"Oh, nothing, nothing at all," answered Emily. She had hoped to have the knot safely tied before the news of her elopement had even reached her father, but she reflected that it could make little difference. He would still be too late to stop her. Eleanor glanced at her niece in perplexity, but her happiness made her anxious to dismiss anything that did not accord with her own sunny humor, and so she did not inquire too closely into the cause of Emily's sudden distress.

It was not, as each lady felt, a day for sitting inside. Eleanor decided that some sort of celebration was necessary and, since she was a woman with all a woman's normal impulses, her celebration took the form of visiting all the most modish shops and purchasing there a collection of bonnets, reticules, silk flowers, and fripperies that left little in her purse but added greatly to her enjoyment.

Emily had accompanied her aunt on this enjoyable expedition, but she had exercised most unwonted caution in her purchases, confining them to a new nightgown and some tooth powder. She worried that these might give Eleanor some clue to her projected elopement, but her aunt was far too taken up with her own concerns to notice. Gaily, she attempted to press Emily to similar extravagances, and when the child would not be urged she insisted on buying a particularly becoming hat for her.

"It is quite a crime not to buy something as becoming to one as that bonnet," she insisted with a laugh. "You must wear it for Simon!"

Emily thanked her with real gratitude, but the kindness made her feel even more guilty at the deception she intended to practice upon her unsuspecting aunt.

The morning having been passed in this satisfactory fashion the two ladies partook of an elegant cold collation and then ordered the carriage to be brought round that they might take a refreshing drive in the Park.

The season had by now got into full swing and the Park was so crowded with fashionable vehicles that progress was made at considerably less than walking pace. Eleanor was hailed by first one and then another of her new friends, who all agreed that she had never been so radiantly lovely nor so fascinating before.

She was happily exchanging witticisms with Lord Melbourne, whose wife was making such a spectacle of herself over Lord Byron, when she suddenly heard her name called out in most unwelcome accents.

"Miss Portland, I say, Miss Portland!" came the well-remembered voice, and turning, she found herself looking straight into the eyes of the Reverend Mr. Higginbottom.

"Good day, Mr. Higginbottom," she said coolly. "What brings you to town?"

The man leered at her in a most annoying manner. "If I said I came for a sight of your sweet face I doubt you would believe me, eh, Miss Portland? No, I have come up on Church business, you know. The thought that I would have the gratification of seeing you, my dear ma'am, was not far from my mind, however!"

Lord Melbourne, who had been eyeing Mr. Higginbottom with some disfavor, now excused himself with a bow and promised himself the pleasure of calling upon her soon. She made a graceful reply and, turning back, was annoyed to see that Mr. Higginbottom had remained and was talking to Emily, who was looking bored.

"Well, I must say, I am surprised to see you in such company, Miss Portland," commenced the gentleman without preamble. "You must feel yourself highly honored by his condescension!"

Since Eleanor had never viewed Lord Melbourne's admiration for her in quite that light she was bereft of speech for a moment. He took her silence for assent and continued to talk of her good fortune.

"Indeed, I can see that you have set yourself up in very good style. I dare swear you will find Pudsley dull enough when you return. However, you will very soon get into your old ways again, I am sure. We shall be happy to see you."

She stared at him in astonishment. He seemed completely to have forgotten the circumstances of their last meeting. "You must know how greatly I am looking forward to having you once more in my little flock," he said significantly.

This last remark was too much. Eleanor found her tongue. "I am desolated to have to disappoint you, sir, but I shall not be returning to Pudsley at all. I have other plans."

"Why, how is this? Lord Portland mentioned nothing to me of this! I saw him but a se'nnight ago."

"Possibly my brother felt that my movements were no concern of yours, Mr. Higginbottom."

"Hardly, ma'am, for the occasion was of my asking his permission to pay my addresses to you," answered the pompous cleric with a leer.

"You asked my brother...Good heavens!" exclaimed Eleanor faintly.

Emily, who had been an interested observer of this little scene, was here betrayed into a giggle. Eleanor's own lips twitched in sympathy, but she frowned at the child and composed her own expression. It was a measure of how her sojourn in London had healed her that she found food for amusement in the situation rather than the old humiliation.

"And what did my brother answer you?" she asked interestedly.

"Oh, he gave us his blessing," answered Higginbottom confidently. Actually, his lordship, much embarrassed, had merely said that the Vicar must ask her himself, for he could not say what she might have in her mind.

Eleanor's brows rose. "I am sorry, sir, that anything my brother may have said should have led you into error. Please believe that my answer is and will ever be quite unchanged." With that she unfurled her parasol and commanded the driver to move off, leaving the cleric standing in the road with a very red face.

As they drove out of earshot Emily succumbed to the laughter which had been consuming her. "Oh, Aunt, how stupid he is! As though you would even look at such a creature. Why, even if you were not to marry Lord Merriot you have dozens of admirers better than him!"

"True, but most unbecoming of me to say," replied Eleanor. She was silent for a moment, thinking of how only a few short weeks ago that stupid bumbling cleric had had the power to distress her. Never again would she have to be concerned with the opinions of such as he! It was Merriot who had done this for her, she suddenly realized. It was he who had first freed her from the fear of scandal by making her waltz with him that first night at Almacks. It was he who had given her back her self-respect, had praised her wit and encouraged her to be herself. To live again! How much she owed him. The thought brought a tender smile to her lips. Tonight she would see him. It seemed almost too long to wait!

Yet, even the most tedious waiting comes to an end eventually, and it was not long before Eleanor stood before her mirror pinning a silk rose into her gleaming hair. She had chosen to wear a gown of shimmering gold satin, embellished with much heavy lace. It was cut low across the bosom and the high waist was gathered by a spangled ribbon. A diaphanous scarf across her white shoulders was her only protection against possible chills in the night air, but not for worlds would she have spoiled the devastating effect of her gown with any heavier wraps.

Simon was punctual to his time and before long Eleanor was stepping out of the little boat which had brought them from Westminster into the brilliant light of the thousands of candles which illuminated the famous gardens.

Instinctively she searched the crowd of merrymakers for Merriot's beloved form. She could not see him, but she was not concerned. He knew that she would be partaking of supper in one of the boxes and would have no difficulty in finding her there.

Meanwhile, she was vastly enjoying her first sight of the gardens. She had never been to any entertainment half so elegant. The famous Pavilion was decorated with flowers and colored lights and the many lesser pavilions were similarly decorated but more discreetly lit. She could see many couples taking advantage of their darkness to engage in a sweet if forbidden interlude. She wondered if Merriot would take her to one of these and smiled at the thought. Her thoughts turned to his ardor last night, and she closed her eyes with a little sigh as an almost physical memory swept over her. No question of propriety would serve to keep her out of his arms tonight. Emily must look to Harriet for a chaperone.

That enterprising damsel had managed to ask Simon in an urgent undervoice if all was ready and upon his whispered assurance that it was she was able to turn her attention to the excellent supper he had provided. Still Harriet and her cavalier had not arrived, but even as they were wondering what could have detained them they were seen threading their way through the throng to the box.

"Sorry we are late, old fellow," said Frederick as they approached. "Devilish difficult getting a boat. Everyone is coming here tonight."

"Oh, it does not matter at all now that you are here," declared Emily as Simon rose to welcome Harriet. "We are having the loveliest time. Are we not, Aunt Eleanor?"

Eleanor nodded, but her bloom had begun to fade a little. Perhaps he too was having difficulty in getting a boat. "What time is it. Simon?" she asked in what she hoped was an indifferent tone.

"Half past nine. ma'am. The fireworks will start at ten. You will enjoy those. Emily."

"Yes, I am sure I shall," she replied.

Presently they finished supper and Simon suggested that they take a stroll about the gardens until the fireworks should begin. Eleanor was loath to leave the box, but then she reflected that if Merriot could not find her then it was quite his own fault for being so tardy and, in any event, she did not care in the least.

It was far from pleasant for Miss Portland to be obliged to play gooseberry to the young couples when she would very much rather have been wandering alone through the gardens on Lord Merriot's arm, but they certainly could not complain that she was a strict duenna that evening. In fact, she very soon lost sight of them altogether so deep was she in her own thoughts, and when she looked around for her companions she was dismayed to find that she was quite alone. It was not a situation that appealed to her. The gardens were full of single gentlemen who, under the protection of their masks, were ready to address any unwary female with a freedom they would never normally have used. She was at first startled and then annoyed to find herself accosted several times. Most of these gentlemen were easily got rid of, however, and she was not seriously discomposed until she turned, vainly trying to regain her box, into a particularly shaded and solitary alleyway. A figure seemed to appear from nowhere at her side.

"Whither are you bound, my pretty wanderer?" asked her assailant in a soft voice.

"I am looking for my friends, who are certainly quite near," answered Eleanor coldly. "Please allow me to pass."

"But I am all alone, and such a night as this was not meant for loneliness. Will you not keep me company for a while?" he replied, catching hold of one of her hands.

"I have told you, sir, that I am with my friends. Let me go at once!" she cried angrily.

For an answer he jerked her into his arms. She felt his breath, rancid with wine, upon her cheek. "No need to run away, sweetheart," he muttered, gripping her so hard that she knew she would carry the marks of his fingers. His lips came down hard upon hers. She jerked her head away and struggled wildly in his arms. She heard him laugh and his grip tightened. "Let me go! Let me go, I tell you!" she cried, in real fear this time. Still he laughed deep in his throat and fastened his lips to hers once more.

She had one hand free and desperately she caught hold of his hair, attempting to pull up his head, but he ignored her tugging. She did not know what to do. He was getting bolder now, his lips were on her neck and shoulders, his hands slipping the pretty scarf from her smooth arms. Wildly, she put up her hand to her hair and grasped the pin she had used to attach her silken roses. She lifted her hand and brought the sharp point down and into the fleshy hand that roved about her breast. He winced, cursed, and his hold on her relaxed. Stopping only to kick her attacker in the shins, she ran off down the alley, leaving him feeling far too sorry for himself to pursue her.

She ran blindly, for there were tears in her eyes and she had by now lost all sense of direction. Dimly, she could see a small pavilion at the end of the path. She made for it, hoping that she might find there someone who could direct her to the main part of the gardens. As she came nearer she saw that there were two people standing in the little shelter, a man and a woman. His head was bent to listen to her; she was standing very close to him. It was just as Eleanor recognized Lord Merriot that Amanda stood on tiptoe and kissed him full on the mouth.

It was too much. She gave a cry which brought up his head in startled inquiry. "Eleanor!" he cried. She gazed at the pair for one piteous moment and then, turning once more, she ran off down the path toward the sounds of music and the lights which danced so merrily above the revelers.

Meanwhile, Simon and Emily had taken advantage of Eleanor's absence to make their escape from the ball. When Eleanor reached the box she found only Harriet and Montgomery seated there. Harriet explained, in an oddly constrained manner, that Emily had been struck by one of her headaches and, as Eleanor was nowhere to be found, Simon had escorted her home. Eleanor was too distracted to notice anything strange in Harriet's manner and instead of the questions that they dreaded the young couple found that Eleanor seemed quite uninterested in her niece or her headache. Instead, she begged to be taken home herself. Harriet, whose enjoyment had already been spoiled by the part she had been forced to play, was only too happy to leave. The ball had hardly started but none of them felt any inclination to linger. As they rose to leave Eleanor caught sight of Merriot making his way toward the box and turned pale.

"Montgomery, please make haste," she cried urgently. "I cannot explain, but we must leave at once!"

He did his best, but Harriet mislaid her reticule and the door of the box stuck in a confoundedly inconvenient manner. Merriot had reached them long before they were ready to leave.

"Eleanor, I must speak to you!" he said in an urgent undertone.

"I have nothing to say to you, my lord," she told him bitterly. "Please go."

"But, my darling, let me explain," he pleaded, his eyes fixed on her face in longing.

She caught her breath on a sob. "Oh, why can you not leave me alone? Have I not suffered enough?"

He bit his lip. "It was not what you think, Eleanor. Will you listen to me?"

She eyed him levelly. "I have listened to you too many times already, my lord."

"I say, sir," interrupted Montgomery diffidently. "If Miss Portland does not want to talk to you then it is not the act of a gentleman to detain her. We were on the point of leaving."

He encountered a look that startled him. Harriet gave a little cry of warning, but she need not have been concerned. Merriot remembered where he was and dropped his fists. "I beg pardon, ma'am." He bowed to Harriet. Then to Eleanor he said, "Farewell until we meet again, my love."

"Good-bye," she answered and swept from the box.

By the time she reached her own chamber the pride that had sustained her would no longer serve to keep back the tears. She fell onto her bed in an agony of weeping and cried until there were no more tears left in her. She acknowledged to herself that she still needed him desperately although he had proved himself forever unworthy of her love. The pain of loss mixed with bitter disillusion was almost more than she could bear. Slowly, as one who is infinitely tired, she disrobed and unbound her hair. Then she sat huddled in a chair near the fire and, staring into its leaping depths, she painfully rehearsed every moment that they had ever spent together.

• • •

Lord Merriot had left the gardens shortly after Eleanor's party. He was furiously angry, with himself, with Amanda, but mostly with Eleanor. Once again he felt that her faith had not been strong enough. Conscious that there had been nothing but gratitude in Amanda's kiss he quite failed to see how it must have appeared to Eleanor. Nor did he know anything of the previous attack which had so thrown her off balance. He only knew that he had no intention of letting the matter rest. He would force her to admit that she had wronged him and then he would leave her to contemplate her folly.

He discovered he had wandered into Grosvenor Square. Her house was but a few steps away. Perhaps the wine had gone to his head a little, perhaps his anger had made him unusually reckless. Whatever the reason, he made for the house without stopping to think of the consequences. When he reached the door he beat a resounding tattoo.

He was answered by a sleepy footman who regarded this unexpected visitor with surprise and suspicion.

"And what might you want, my fine fellow?" he demanded, peering into the darkness. "Oh, it is you, my lord. I beg pardon. I did not recognize your honor at first."

Merriot was popular with the staff, for he was generous with his money and any menial performing a service for him might be sure of a gold coin for himself. Moreover, the whole servants' hall knew that Lord Merriot was sweet on Miss Portland. The man was shocked, however, when the visitor calmly announced that he wished to see her immediately.

"But 'tis past midnight, sir, and Miss has been in her chamber this hour or more."

"Has she indeed?" Merriot slipped a hand into his pocket and brought forth a handful of gleaming coins. He allowed them to slip from one hand to the other so that the man could see them clearly. There were ten in all.

"Nevertheless, I would like to speak with her. Perhaps you could just leave the door open and contrive to forget that you saw me tonight?" suggested Merriot casually.

The man swallowed. "I daren't, my lord. Really, I daren't," he averred.

Merriot smiled and added another coin to his collection. The sight of so much money, more than six months' pay, was too much for the man. He grabbed at the coins and deliberately turned his back as Merriot strode past him and into the hallway.

"Quick, man, which is her room?" he demanded in a low voice.

"Up the stairs and first door to the right," replied the footman and watched in some astonishment as his lordship ran lightly up the stairs. Shaking his head over the strange ways of the Quality which shocked an honest fellow, he sank back onto his bench and began to count the gleaming coins in his hand.

chapter 12

Eleanor was still huddled in her chair when she heard his knock upon her door. She lifted her head.

"Is that you, Emily?" she called. There was no reply, but the handle turned and the door swung open. Merriot stood upon the threshold. She stared at him, shocked and bewildered.

"What . . . what are you doing here?" she demanded. "What do you want?"

He had come prepared to fling at her all the hurt and anger she had caused him, but one glance at her tragic face and all such thoughts vanished.

"My dear," he said, moving toward her with his hands held out to her. "My dear love, will you not listen to me now?"

"Oh, how dare you?" she cried passionately. "What do you think of me that you come here in the middle of the night? Do you expect me to forget everything that has passed and just fall into your arms? Go back to Amanda if that is what you are looking for! Judging by what I saw tonight she will be delighted to receive you!"

He smiled at her in a most disturbing way. "My little love, do not be ridiculous. If you had stayed but a moment longer you would have seen Amanda depart. I did not ask for her embraces."

"Oh, yes, I saw how you struggled. What were you doing there with her in any event if it was all as innocent as you say?" she demanded angrily.

"It is really very simple. Amanda needed money urgently. I could not refuse her, it would have been ungentlemanly. As for that kiss, it was merely gratitude on her part. Amanda has no more interest in me than I have in her now. She has replaced me easily enough."

"No matter, you will soon find another lady to accommodate you," she flung at him.

He laughed, advancing across the bedchamber toward her. "Eleanor, my sweet love. Do you have any idea how beautiful you are? I have never seen your lovely hair unbound before." He reached out to take one of her long tresses in his hand. She jerked her head away and retreated behind a small sofa.

"Do not come near me!" she cried warningly.

"Why? What will you do now?" he asked, calmly removing the sofa from his path.

"I will scream," she told him breathlessly, backing toward the bed.

He came up to her. She could retreat no further. He took her chin in his hand and forced her face up to his. "Scream, then, my darling, for I have no intention of going anywhere!"

She might have done so had not his lips stifled the sounds. He held her so for a long time, his mouth gentle yet demanding. In spite of herself her lips parted under his mouth and her body swayed toward him. The huge mother-of-pearl buttons that adorned his coat bit into her soft flesh but as he pressed her even closer she did not cry out but instead flung her arms around his neck with a sob of gladness.

When they finally broke apart they gazed at each other in a kind of helpless longing. "We . . . I . . . I cannot, Robert!" she whispered despairingly.

"I will not force you to it, my dearest," he answered softly, reaching out his hand to caress the slender column of her throat.

"Ah! . . . do not . . . ," she begged as the gentle hand slowly moved over her shoulders and rested upon her breast. He was breathing heavily, his eyes burning into her through the thin muslin of the robe.

"Eleanor?" he said, very softly.

"I am afraid, Robert."

"Of me?" he murmured.

"No...I...Robert, do not ask me to do this! Oh, my darling!" She could withhold herself no longer. He caught her roughly in his arms and she answered him passion for passion. She reveled in the warmth of his lips upon her flesh, the feel of his muscular body against her own. His hands were fumbling at the ribbons of her gown, but he grew impatient and tore the flimsy stuff so that her garment fell from her, leaving her naked in his encircling arms.

"Darling...oh, my darling...," he murmured as he gazed at the beauties of her slender form. She smiled at him, offering herself plainly, without words.

He picked her up, his arms trembling, and laid her upon the bed. She lay watching him as he quickly stripped off his coat and shirt. His body was strongly muscled yet lean. She reached out a hand to touch the firm skin and he jumped as though her touch had burned him.

"My God, Eleanor, there has never been a woman like you," he told her as his hands explored her soft, scented skin.

She held out her arms and pulled him down to her, her lips seeking his with all the hunger that she had been forced to suppress for ten long years. There, in the blaze of candlelight, Merriot cast out forever the memory of that other forgotten lover, for she realized now that she had not known what love could really be until she lay in his arms.

It was dawn. He turned to her, his head resting upon her shoulder.

"My love, if I am to leave without being seen I should go," he told her.

"Yes, I suppose you should," she replied, but she showed no inclination to release him from her embrace.

He watched her for a while, lovingly noting every line of her lovely face and the way that her hair tumbled in unruly curls over her forehead. "You do not regret this, Eleanor? I should not have taken such advantage of you, I know, but my darling it was worth it!"

She kissed him tenderly on the mouth. "It was very wrong of you, sweetheart, but then I so much wanted you to do it. I regret nothing but that you must leave my side, even for a moment."

"It will not be for long, my love. We have nothing to wait for. Let us be married within the month!"

She nestled closer. "I should like that."

Halfheartedly, he attempted to rise. "I must go!"

"Yes, Robert," she agreed, nuzzling his cheek.

"Eleanor! You must let me go. It is your reputation I am thinking of!" he protested laughingly.

For an answer she pressed closer, his arms closed tightly around her once again.

When she awoke there was bright sunshine streaming into her room. The bed beside her was empty. Dimly she remembered that he had awakened her and gently kissed her good-bye. "I have to go out of town today, my love, on business, but I shall come to you as soon as I return this evening," he had whispered.

Then she must have fallen asleep again, for the clock upon the mantel told her that it was twelve noon. She stretched contentedly, her thoughts returning to that sweet, secret love they had shared. She knew that as a lady she should be tormented with guilt, shedding tears of remorse, but instead she felt better than she had in years. A quick glance in the mirror told her that her skin was rosy and her eyes bright. Love, she decided, was a wonderful cosmetic. Then she giggled a little as she thought of what the Reverend Higginbottom and his parishioners would say if they could have seen her last night. All their worst suspicions were confirmed, she was happy to reflect.

She would have liked to remain lazily in bed, but she was soon disturbed by her abigail, who announced that Miss Milton was below and wished to speak to her. Eleanor glanced at the girl out of the corner of her eye. Did she know anything of last night? The friendly smile reassured her. In fact, she need not have worried, for Merriot had rewarded the attendant footman generously on his departure and the man had no intention of revealing his part in the night's happenings, which could only lead to his own dismissal.

Harriet was seated nervously upon the edge of her seat when Miss Portland breezed into the room and kissed her affectionately. She felt that she was much to blame for having assisted in her friend's flight, nor did she relish her present role. However, Emily had entrusted to her a letter which was to be delivered the next day and she had promised to give it to Eleanor in person.

"Harriet, my dear, I am pleased that you have called. I must apologize to you for having spoiled your evening last night. I am sure you would have liked to stay for the dancing and I made you leave so soon. Never mind, perhaps we shall go there again sometime soon. Have you seen Emily yet this morning? Or is the child still in her chamber?"

"No, ma'am, I have not seen Emily, and I do not think that she is in her chamber, either. In fact, I know that she is not!" answered Harriet in a voice of doom.

"Good heavens, Harriet, what are you talking about?" demanded Eleanor, taken aback.

Miss Milton held out the letter. Eleanor took it with a questioning look and quickly ripped it open.

My dear aunt, Emily had written. *By the time you read this I shall be already far away. I am sorry to do this but you must see that it is not at all fair that Simon and I should not be able to marry because of something that happened years and years ago. He will take very good care of me, so do not worry. Your loving niece, Emily.*

Eleanor sat down rather suddenly. "Harriet, did you know of this?"

The girl nodded miserably.

"Then you did wrong not to tell me of it before. Oh, I know very well that you did not wish to betray a friend, but you have no idea how much harm may come of this. I daresay you all think it very romantic, but it is merely grossly improper, as Emily will soon find out."

Harriet's eyes filled with tears. "I did tell her so, indeed I did, Miss Portland. She was quite determined. What will you do?"

"What can I do? I must assume that they have set off for Scotland. They will be halfway there by now!"

"No, ma'am, I do not think so, for there was no moon last night, and they could not have traveled far without it. They will have put up somewhere nearby and left this morning," replied Harriet sensibly.

"If that is so, then it might be possible to catch them. They are traveling in a hired chaise, I presume?"

"Yes, I think so."

"Good! Then a sporting curricle might easily catch them.

I must send for Merriot, for I have not a penny to my name until next quarter's allowance. Besides, we need a man for this!"

She was about to dash off a note to Merriot when she suddenly remembered his whispered words. He was out of town today! Now what?

"Stay, Harriet. Does Lennox know of this flight?" she demanded.

Harriet shook her head. "Simon would not leave word for his father. He said he would not be missed."

"Very well, then, I shall send to the Viscount. It is his responsibility to go after his son!"

She had a note conveyed to the Lennox mansion, which was situated only a few streets away, and waited with considerable impatience for a reply. She could not bring herself to talk with the unhappy Harriet, with whom she was seriously annoyed, but sat worrying about her niece until a peremptory knock at the front door roused her. A few moments later Viscount Lennox was ushered into the room.

"May I know, ma'am, what is the meaning of this note?" he demanded without preamble.

"I had thought it to be sufficiently clear," she replied coldly. "Your son has eloped with my niece. Due entirely, I might add, to your ridiculous handling of the affair."

Each had forgotten Harriet's interested presence. The Viscount answered her furiously. "If I had known that my son had become involved with a young woman so lost to all propriety as to lend herself to such an adventure, I should have taken greater pains to keep them apart!"

"Like aunt, like niece!" Eleanor flashed back at him. "You seemed to think less about propriety ten years ago!"

"Eleanor, I did not mean to say . . . ! You misunderstood me!"

"I think not, sir! However, this vulgar quarreling does not get us anywhere. I think that there is still a good chance that we might catch up with them if we leave now. Will you assist me to undo whatever harm this escapade might cause?"

"What do you want me to do?" he asked wearily.

"Why, go after them, of course!" she cried. "If we can find them then I shall escort Emily home and I shall be able to say that we have merely been visiting and that you and Simon have been kind enough to escort us. No one will think that odd,

which they might if they were to see Emily being dragged back
in tears in your company."

He stared at her. "You wish to come, too?" he asked incredulously.

"Lennox, this is no time to be worrying about the past.
These young people must be prevented from making a mistake
that they may regret for the rest of their lives. You know as
well as I the kind of scandal that such an elopement will pro-
voke."

"You will trust yourself to me?" he asked softly.

"Do not be a fool," she answered shortly. "Are you driving
your grays?"

"Certainly," he nodded.

"Good. Then let us be off!" she said briskly. "Harriet, you
are to go home and tell as many people as you can that Emily
and I are visiting friends in the country under the escort of
Lord Lennox and Mr. Trafford."

Half an hour later, Eleanor, having changed into a very
smart traveling costume of dove-gray wool with which she
carried an enormous swan's-down muff, climbed gracefully
into the sporting vehicle. The groom let go of the four dancing
thoroughbreds and they started forward, daintily picking their
way through the afternoon traffic.

Eleanor did not notice the face at the window that watched
her departure with a satisfied smile, nor did she observe the
dark beauty whose carriage they passed and who stared after
the couple in open amazement. Lady Amanda could think of
no innocent reason to account for this escapade in Merriot's
future wife, but she soon forgot the incident when she arrived
at the house of her new lover.

The traffic was heavy until they cleared the city and pro-
ceeded through the little village of Islington. From there they
were able to pick up the trail of the fugitives by stopping at
every inn upon the road north. At St. Albans they were fortunate. A couple answering to their description had passed
through the town not four hours earlier.

"Not bad," said the Viscount. "We should be able to make
up the time. If I know hired chaises they will have trouble
getting the boys to spring their horses."

By this time it was past four and Eleanor was conscious that
she had partaken of nothing all day but a hurried cup of coffee
at an inn just outside Highgate. "Pray, could we stop for some

food, sir? I am not inclined to starve to death for the sake of those naughty children!"

"I beg your pardon, ma'am. We will rest here for a while. They will not be so foolish as to travel all night. They, too, will have to rest."

"Frankly, sir, at this moment I do not care in the least. Please let us eat!"

Once more the Viscount was disconcerted by Miss Portland's unexpectedly prosaic side. That she should be thinking of food at a time like this! He did not know what to make of her.

While he was still wondering she had leaped down from the curricle, disdaining his proffered arm, and had walked into the hostelry, scattering orders around her. He had nothing to do but meekly follow her into the wainscoted parlor where a good fire blazed in the grate.

Eleanor was standing before it holding out one elegantly shod foot to the blaze. "I have ordered dinner, sir. I hope it will be to your liking," she said composedly.

"Thank you. I am sure it will be adequate," he answered, nettled.

She raised her delicate brows. "You are cross, sir, and no doubt chilled. Will you not warm yourself by the fire?"

He did not smile, but he followed her advice. A good dinner, comprised of a leg of lamb, a dish of boiled carrots, a pigeon pie, two side dishes of ox tongue in oyster sauce, and a dish of mumbled rabbit soon restored his temper, however, particularly as it was washed down by a glass of rare port.

"I will take a glass of wine with you, sir," said Eleanor as she sat leaning her elbows upon the table.

"Port is hardly a lady's drink, ma'am," replied his lordship stiffly.

"You know, Richard, you have grown awfully stuffy over the years," she told him thoughtfully. "I had no notion you would become so conventional."

He flushed. "I am sorry if I offend you, ma'am. Certainly I will pour a glass for you if you wish it."

"Oh, I do, Richard, I do," she assured him with a chuckle.

They sat sipping in silence for a few moments. "I think that we should be getting on now if we are to come upon them before nightfall," remarked the Viscount.

"You are very right, sir. Let us be on our way," she replied cordially. "I feel ready for anything now!"

She paused on the way out to compliment the landlord upon his dinner, to which he replied that if he had his way he would cater to none but the Quality, who were so pleasant and open-handed in their ways.

It was by now past five and they were so far from home that it would clearly be impossible to return to London that evening. She refused to consider what must happen if they failed to catch up with the runaways that night.

Fortunately, at the next change they found that the young couple had stopped to dine at the hostelry and had left only half an hour earlier. Obviously, they had no fear of being pursued.

"Only half an hour! My compliments, sir. It is your excellent driving that has allowed us to overtake the children so easily," said Eleanor pleasantly.

She had spoken too soon. In his impatience to be off Lord Lennox miscalculated a particularly difficult bend in the road and Miss Portland found herself flung from her seat to land in a tumbled heap on top of her traveling companion. She sat up shakily, her hand to her head.

"Oh, my God," she gasped. "What happened?"

Lord Lennox had already stumbled to his horses' heads and was surveying the damage grimly. "I regret this more than I can say. One of the wheelers is lame and the axle is quite gone. I do not know how we are to continue."

"But is there not a vehicle to be hired?" she demanded, attempting to stand. She swayed and fell to the ground again, dizzy and sick.

"If there were, ma'am, you are in no fit state to travel. We must rest here for the night."

"No, no. We cannot do such a thing. What are you thinking of?" she cried agitatedly.

"We have little choice. It is late and you are unfit to travel."

"Is there not another inn? We cannot stay in the same house. You must see that!"

He bowed. "I will inquire. I suggest that you go in. You are quite done up!" Indeed she was very pale and shaken by the accident. The innkeeper's wife, a motherly soul, bustled out of the house to assist her into the private parlor.

"There you are, my dearie. Just you sit quiet an' I'll bring you a nice cup of chocolate. Then you'll be as right as rain. It is a terrible corner that, something ought to be done about it. We've 'ad that many accidents there, I can tell you." Eleanor reflected that it would take more than a cup of chocolate to sort out this dreadful tangle. She had dashed off in such a fine fervor to save her niece from disgrace and instead she had once more risked her own reputation for no good cause. And what of Merriot? He had assured her that he would call upon her that evening. What would he think when he found that she was not there to receive him? Her head ached abominably and her muscles were stiff from the long hours of jolting over the roadways.

She glanced up as the door opened and Lennox came into the room. "I thought it best to tell the landlord that you are my sister," he informed her. "The situation might seem a little odd otherwise. I am afraid there is not another inn. This is hardly a village that could support two; it is little more than a hamlet."

"Very well, sir, I am your sister, then," she answered in a tired voice.

The landlady arrived with chocolate for Eleanor and a bottle of brandy for his lordship, whose fashionable attire and haughty demeanor had greatly impressed the good lady.

"An' when you're finished you just ring the bell and I'll take you up to your room. You look worn out, you poor dear," she said.

Eleanor thanked her with a sweet smile that quite won her heart. Lennox, who was glad of the brandy, noticed some color stealing back into her cheeks.

"You are looking better, Eleanor," he commented.

"Thank you, Richard," she said, sipping her chocolate. "This is a sorry tangle, is it not?"

"It would be if news of it should get out, but that is unlikely. When you return to town you may say that you have been visiting friends. That is all."

"That is if my brother, who should be home tomorrow, does not start a hue and cry after me, and Emily, too. What will he think when he finds us both gone? Something of this is bound to become known."

"Let us hope not," he replied, pouring himself another glass.

They sat in silence for a while. He watched her covertly, wondering about the change in her. Despite her fatigue there was still an aura of happiness about her; last night's rapture had left its mark upon her face. He thought that never, even in her first season, had she looked more beautiful nor more desirable than she did at that moment in her dusty habit. His eyes lingered upon her mouth, remembering what it had been like to kiss the soft lips. Perhaps the brandy was partly responsible for what happened, but quite suddenly he could restrain himself no longer. In an instant Eleanor found herself seized and clasped in his arms.

"Richard, have you taken leave of your senses!" she exclaimed, attempting to push him away.

"No, by God, I think I have just come to them. Eleanor, you belong to me; I should never have let you go all those years ago." With that he bent his head and kissed her in very much the same way Merriot had kissed her the previous night. This time she felt no similar desire to respond but struggled in his arms, and when he still did not release her she had recourse to her most potent weapon and burst into tears.

Startled, he released her. "Forgive me, Eleanor, but I did not think that I was as distasteful to you as all that!"

"Well, you are!" she declared pettishly.

"You did not think so once," he retorted angrily.

"How dare you bring all that up again? I have grown up a good deal since those days, Lennox. One of the things I have learned is that no man of real honor would seduce a girl almost young enough to be his daughter, nor, having done so, would any power on earth be sufficient to take her from his protection! Now I know what a real and true love can be I realize that what you offered me was nothing but a weak and lustful passion!"

"You will be sorry you spoke to me in this way!" said Lennox threateningly.

"Why, do you intend to rape me?" she demanded with a scornful laugh.

Her laughter bruised his vanity even more than her words. He made a grab at her but she was too quick for him. She ran across the room to the fireplace and picked up a large and heavy fire-iron.

"If you come one step closer I will use this," she told him breathlessly.

He laughed unpleasantly. "You could not. Put that stupid thing down, Eleanor." He moved toward her, his eyes resting on her flushed countenance. "Do you know how alluring you are, my dear?" he asked softly.

"Of course!" she answered and flung the fire-iron at his head.

A childhood spent in games with the village children had trained her eye and her aim was excellent. Her adversary went down in a crumpled heap at her feet and lay there, a little blood seeping from the wound in his temple.

"Oh, my God!" cried Eleanor. "What am I to do now?"

She bethought her of the kind landlady. Staunching the blood as best she could with her handkerchief, she left him and rang the bell for assistance. When the good lady arrived she told her that her brother had been more seriously hurt by the accident than they had at first thought. He must be conveyed to his room. If the landlady thought there was anything odd about this she said nothing, but her quick eyes had noted the fire-iron, which still lay where it had fallen. It was not for her to question the Quality or she might have wanted to know what had possessed the lady to strike her *brother* thus. Instead she called two large and witless young men out of the taproom and had his lordship tenderly conveyed to his chamber.

Eleanor, who was quite worn out, was only too happy to be conducted to her own chamber, where a warm bed awaited her. She thanked the landlady with real gratitude for her help, closed the door behind her, and after a moment's thought turned the key in the lock. She then prepared herself as best she could to retire. She had been obliged to borrow certain essentials from her hostess, whose nightgown was at once too short and too wide for her, but she donned it gratefully and clambered into bed. Just before she blew out the candle she slipped out from under the covers and dragged a heavy carved chair across the room, wedging it under the door handle. With a satisfied air she ran lightly back to the huge old-fashioned bed and snuggled down under the covers. Her last thought was that she must return to London on the morrow with or without the runaways. She did not wish to spend another moment in the company of the man whom she had once loved and for whom she had risked so much.

chapter 13

Although it had never occurred to Lady Amanda to be faithful to any of her many lovers, she was filled with righteous indignation by Eleanor's flight with Lennox. Since Merriot had been so very obliging about her debts she had been quite in charity with him and felt that he had been treated shabbily. She decided that he should be told the truth as soon as possible and felt that in telling him herself she was behaving in a most honorable way. Therefore she once more, much to Weston's dismay, presented herself at the house in St. James, demanding to see his lordship.

"I am very sorry, my lady, but his lordship is out of town." The man bowed respectfully.

"And when do you expect him back?"

"Oh, very late, my lady. There would be no use in waiting, I assure your ladyship."

"Good heavens, man, I have no intention of waiting but you may tell your master when he returns that I have something to tell him that he would give a good deal to know!"

Much relieved at having got rid of her so easily, he murmured, "Very good, my lady," and ushered her toward the door. He was too late. Just as they reached it the door opened and Merriot stood frowning upon the threshhold.

"Amanda!" he exclaimed in annoyance. "What the . . . ?"

She moved toward him impulsively. "Forgive me, Robert, but I thought it my duty to come. I do not intend to make a scene, I promise you."

"Well, what is it? Come, I am tired and exceedingly hungry and am therefore in no mood for your cajolery!"

"My dear, I think that you would rather hear what I have to say in private," she answered with a significant glance toward the waiting manservant.

"Oh, very well. Come into the library. Weston, bring me a bottle of the madeira and order dinner to be set on the table within half an hour. I am famished!"

"Very well, my lord," replied the servant, and hurried off to galvanize the artist in the kitchen who was at that moment putting the finishing touches to a dinner consisting of a roast rib of prime beef, a dish of veal in a cream sauce, some poached oysters, and a dish of cheesecakes. The smells from this modest repast floated gently into the hallway and sharpened his lord-ship's appetite.

"Well, Amanda, out with it. What is it this time?"

"I came only to do you a service, Robert, I swear!"

"Well, that makes a pleasant change," remarked his lord-ship, pouring the wine. "Will you take a glass with me?"

"Thank you." She seemed uncertain of how to discharge her errand. Merriot was more formidable suddenly than she remembered.

"This is difficult for me, Robert. I hope you will believe that I am here because you have been good to me and not out of malice."

He glanced up at her. "I should never suspect you of malice, my dear. It is not one of your vices."

She laughed. "I have enough of those without adding to them. Listen, then, my dear. This afternoon I happened to be driving in my barouche and I chanced to pass down South Audley Street on my way to . . . Well, never mind that."

"Yes, Ravenscar has lodgings in Mount Street, does he not?" interrupted Merriot.

"Very well, since you have guessed it, I was on my way to see him. In any event, at about half past one I saw Miss Eleanor Portland, dressed for traveling, sitting up beside Lennox as large as life. What's more, he had dismissed his groom and had a team harnessed. Now why should he need four horses if he were not planning a long journey?"

Merriot looked stunned. "Are you sure of this?" he demanded.

"My dear, I would not have come here if I had not been quite sure. I do not wish to make mischief, but you had told me that you were going to be married, and I am not mistaken, am I? I assumed that you meant to marry Miss Portland."

"No, you were not mistaken," he said grimly.

"Well, perhaps there is an innocent explanation but I remember that old scandal. Perhaps they are still lovers after all."

Merriot was very pale. "It is not possible! There is some mistake!"

She shrugged. "Very well, go to the house and see for yourself. If she is at home, then I am mistaken and it was all perfectly innocent. If not . . . Well, it is as well to know now what kind of woman she is."

He could not but catch the note of jealousy in her voice. Probably she had blown up the incident out of all proportion out of spite. Yet as he had said, malice was not one of Amanda's characteristics.

"Well, Robert, I shall go now. I did not expect any thanks for this, but I am sorry to see you so overcome. I had not thought any woman had it in her power to subdue you so completely. I admire her for having brought the famous lover to heel!" she said with a laugh.

"I do thank you, Amanda. Not for the news you brought but for your concern. It was a kind impulse, my dear," he told her with an effort.

She stood on tiptoe to kiss his cheek. "I am sorry, my dear. Truly, I am."

He bowed her out of the room, but his mind was already grappling with his problem. He must find Eleanor, for only from her could he learn the truth. What he would do then he was not sure. Still he clung to hope. Amanda may have been mistaken. Eleanor might be waiting for him even now. He would not allow himself to believe anything else.

He arrived in South Audley Street just as Eleanor, having protected her virtue with the aid of a poker, was sinking into a deep sleep in the tiny village just north of St. Albans. Fiskin informed Merriot in a worried voice that he had seen neither

Miss Portland nor Miss Emily for several hours and was wondering what he ought to do.

Merriot brushed Emily's absence aside. He was interested only in Eleanor's whereabouts.

"Well, sir, I did not see Miss Eleanor leave the house myself, but I know that the housekeeper, Mrs. Burrows, did, my lord," offered the butler.

"Then please ask Mrs. Burrows if she would be kind enough to come here. I should like to ask her a few questions."

The housekeeper, when she arrived, was obviously big with news. She had hated Eleanor ever since the trouble over Lucy; it gave her great pleasure to be the one to tell her fine gentleman the truth about her.

"Mrs. Burrows, come in," said Merriot, striving to appear unconcerned. The woman caught the strain under his calm manner and smiled to herself. "I believe you may be able to shed some light on this mystery."

"There is no mystery that I know of, my lord," she responded. "Early this afternoon, Miss Portland had a note taken round to Viscount Lennox's house. He came himself and they went off together. That is all I know."

"She sent for him?" repeated Merriot incredulously.

"Oh, yes, sir. The gentleman has not visited her above once before. He would not have come if she had not wanted him," she averred.

"I see! Do you have any idea where they may have gone?" he demanded.

She smiled primly. "Well, I did take the liberty of questioning Hugo, the footman who handed Miss into the carriage. He said that he heard the Great North Road mentioned. I don't know, I am sure, why they should be going up north when Lord Portland is expected here only tomorrow."

This news conveyed a ray of hope to Lord Merriot. Why she should have chosen Lennox as her escort he did not begin to understand, but if they were traveling north, then perhaps she had had some news from home that would account for her sudden departure. Still he was not satisfied. Only one course could answer. He must follow them.

Eleanor awoke the next morning with a feeling that something disagreeable awaited her. At first she could not remember where she was, but as sleep receded she realized that what she had at first thought was nightmare had actually happened.

She rang the bell and requested breakfast in her room. She had no intention of facing Lord Lennox until she had gathered her wits about her. When she did eventually appear in the little parlor, he jumped up quickly with an embarrassed air and stood there looking as sheepish as a schoolboy.

"Eleanor, I . . . I . . . You must forgive me for what happened last night. It was that cursed brandy, I think. You know that I would never have forced you to . . . Please, can you not forget what happened?"

She sighed. "I am sorry, my lord, but I do not think I can forget it quite as easily as that. I think it would be best if you were to take me home. Now that the children have been together for two nights and a day, it makes little sense to try to stop their marriage. I fear Emily's reputation will be damaged beyond repair whatever we do. Let us return to London. I must face my brother with this news. I have betrayed his trust in me and I shall never forgive myself!"

He bowed his head in acquiescence. She picked up her reticule and moved across the room to the mirror, placing her bonnet over her curls at a becoming angle. "For what do we wait, sir?" she asked with raised brows.

He roused himself and strode out of the inn. It was a bright, sunny morning and Eleanor's spirits rose a little as she stepped into the courtyard after him. As she did so, a sporting curricle, drawn by a team of sweating chestnuts, swept into the courtyard, spattering mud as it screeched to a halt.

The gentleman who jumped down from this equipage was in no very good temper. He had been driving all night and had disturbed the rest of a great many honest innkeepers by his progress. He had been able to follow them easily enough; everyone remembered the handsome gentleman and his lovely lady. He knew the road and had guessed that they must have stopped for the night in the area. This was the fourth inn he had tried. Now he had found her and instead of relief he felt only an overwhelming anger.

"So, madame, I find you here. I would not credit it when I was told, but after all, you are so much in the habit of this kind of thing, I cannot think why I should have been surprised."

Eleanor gasped. She hardly recognized her tender lover in

this harsh-faced man who flung insults at her as though they were blows.

"Robert, what on earth are you doing here? Why are you talking to me like this?" she cried.

"You can ask that when I find you here alone with Lennox, of all men! You must think me very stupid!"

"But . . . Oh, you cannot think . . . Robert, you do not understand!"

"It seems clear enough, madame. Did you spend the night in this inn?"

"Yes, I did, but . . ."

"And Lennox? Where did he spend the night?"

"Here, but . . ."

"You need say no more. I wish I understood why you felt it necessary to add me to your conquests but no matter. You have now obviously obtained your real desire."

She gave a cry of pain. "Robert, you cannot believe that! Nothing happened between us. Nothing!"

"Do you really expect me to believe that?" he sneered.

"I expect you to believe me, sir," interrupted Lennox.

An ugly look swept over Merriot's face. "So you have a tongue, do you? I had thought you intended to shelter behind this lady's skirts all day!"

The Viscount started forward, his fists raised.

"No! No!" cried Eleanor, flinging herself between the two men. "There is no need for this! Robert, nothing happened! Please, please believe me!"

Neither man paid the slightest heed to this. The jealousy of one and the frustrated passion of the other deafened them to her cries. "Step to one side, madame, or you will be hurt," instructed Merriot brusquely.

Although Lord Lennox was a member of the fashionable set and occasionally sparred with his cronies at Jackson's famous saloon, he was no match for an acknowledged Corinthian. Merriot, as even Eleanor could see at a glance, was an expert in the art. Lennox could not stand long against the furious onslaught of blows. Besides, he was the elder by several years. She watched as again and again Merriot planted a hit upon that handsome countenance. Suddenly she could bear it no longer. She flung herself at Merriot. As she did so his right hand came up in a punishing blow which caught her full on her shapely chin. She gave a startled cry and crumpled in a heap at his feet.

"My God! Eleanor, my darling!" he cried, dropping on his knees beside her prostrate form.

"I think you have killed her!" exclaimed Lennox, wiping the blood from his mouth. Certainly she looked deathly pale, but the faint rise and fall of her breast showed that she still lived.

"Don't just stand there, you fool, get some brandy!" ordered Merriot, cradling her figure in his arms.

Much as he resented the tone in which the order was given, Lennox hurried into the taproom to procure some of the life-giving liquid. When he returned, he found that Miss Portland had opened her eyes, but she still seemed dazed. Merriot took the glass from his hand and held it to her lips, forcing the fiery liquid down her throat. She coughed and spluttered, but enough of the stimulant went down to bring some color back into her cheeks.

With returning strength came remembrance. She discovered that she was lying in Merriot's arms and thrust him away as though his touch contaminated her. "Let me go! Do not touch me!" she cried weakly.

"Eleanor, listen to me. It does not matter about last night. I can forgive you anything if you will only come back to me!" declared Merriot, seizing her hand.

"How dare you? You came galloping in here, called me a harlot or as good as, and now you want me to forget every insult and allow you to forgive me for something that never occurred except in your own imagination. Well, let me tell you, sir, that I can do without your forgiveness. I did not spend the night in my lover's arms as you seem to think! For the very good reason that I thought I was in love with you!"

"Eleanor!"

"Now, however, my eyes are opened to your true character, and I can only say that I hope I may never set eyes on either of you as long as I live. And what is more, I utterly refuse to travel home with either of you!"

"But, my dear, you must get home somehow," expostulated Lennox. He encountered a look from Merriot.

"I will thank you not to call my future wife 'Dear,'" said that gentleman dangerously.

"I am not your future wife. I am not anyone's future wife!" declared Eleanor furiously.

"You see, sir?" said Lennox with some satisfaction.

"If you do not wish me to finish my work on you, be silent!" snapped Merriot. "Eleanor, be sensible. Let me convey you to London and we can discuss all this when you are feeling calmer."

She could have screamed with vexation. "Do not assume that reasonable tone with me. I am not a child! When I say I do not want to see you anymore, that is exactly what I mean!"

"Permit me to escort you, Eleanor," interposed Lennox with a bow.

"After the way you behaved last night, sir, I wonder you can suggest it," she replied with spirit.

Merriot's ears pricked up at that. "Why? What happened last night?"

She was sorry to have said so much. "Nothing, let it alone."

"On the contrary, I think his lordship should know the truth," said Lennox. "It will interest you, my lord."

"Go on," said Merriot briefly.

Lennox gave a wry smile. "It redounds little to my credit, but I think you ought to know that the lady whom you have accused of being my mistress last night went so far as to fight me off with a poker. I still bear the mark, as you can see."

"And why did the lady find it necessary to strike you with a poker?" asked Merriot with dangerous calm.

He shrugged. "I fear the intoxication of her presence was too much for me. Also, I was under the misapprehension that her rejection of me stemmed from pride and anger. I did not know what is now quite obvious to me, that her affections have been engaged elsewhere."

"Nevertheless, you shall answer to me for the attempt!" declared Merriot harshly.

"Do not be ridiculous. There has been enough fighting already," interrupted Eleanor. "Reflect, my lord, that this gentleman merely attempted to do what you did yourself the other night. The difference lay in my reception of your advances, not in any superiority of motive in yourself!"

"How can you say that! I want to marry you!" he cried.

"As I do," interjected Lennox swiftly.

She stared at him. "That is ridiculous, Richard. You still have a wife. Nothing has changed."

"Indeed it has. Simon is almost of age. He could no longer be hurt by the scandal if I divorce his mother. I, too, have changed. I no longer fear the world's opinion as I did."

"Well, I am very grateful to you both, but as I said before, I have no intention of marrying anyone. Now if I am not to fall into strong hysterics, I will ask you both, once more, to leave me alone!"

"Certainly not!" answered both men simultaneously. "Eleanor, you are in no condition to manage alone," continued Merriot. "Please allow me to take you home."

"No!" she almost shrieked. "I shall travel by post. That is . . . Oh, I forgot! I have no money. What am I going to do?"

The dispute might have gone on all day had it not come to a sudden end when a post chaise rolled noisily into their midst. It came to a halt and the windows were let down. "Good heavens, Father! What are you doing here?" exclaimed a well-known voice. Lennox found himself staring incredulously into the merry eyes of his missing son.

chapter 14

There was a stunned silence, then everyone started talking at once.

"Simon! Good God, what are you doing here?" cried Lord Lennox in complete amazement.

"Where is Emily?" demanded Eleanor at the same moment. Mr. Trafford did not answer immediately, however, for he had by now noticed the blood which still trickled sluggishly from his father's lip.

"What has been happening here?" he demanded. "Miss Portland, you look ill. Is there anything that I can do for you?"

"Yes, there is!" she answered with some asperity. "You may tell me where you have taken Emily."

Simon looked a little sheepish. "Well, to tell you the truth, I took her to Great-aunt Letty's."

"You have taken her to your aunt? But whatever for? Surely you are not married already?"

"Well, no, we are not married yet. You see, Emily was quite determined on this elopement, but I've been on the town long enough to know that this sort of thing just ain't done. There was no convincing Emily, though, so I agreed to go off

with her. I had to deceive her a little. I told her we were going
to Gretna, but I took her to Crawley Place instead. Aunt Letty
managed to convince her that the whole thing was quite improper, but Emily is to stay with her until you see reason,
Father, and give your consent to our marriage."

The Viscount shrugged. "I can hardly refuse, can I? If you
do not marry the child, she will be ruined. I am not so callous.
You are honor-bound to marry her."

Simon seemed offended. "Not at all, Father. Do you think
I would not take better care of my Emily than that? The first
night we spent with Nanny Wilson, and you don't know Nanny
if you think she would allow any... Well, you know what I
mean. And last night we were at my aunt's, so there has been
no harm done at all as far as I can see!"

Eleanor held out her hand. "Simon, you have done very
well. I only hope that this has taught that naughty child a
lesson. As for you, my lords, I need no longer trouble you with
my welfare. I am sure that Simon will convey me back to the
city in the greatest comfort."

"I should be happy, ma'am, of course." The young man
bowed. He was looking, with some amazement, at the spectacle
of his elegant father bearing all the signs of one who has just
been engaged in a mill. Moreover, he could see from where
he stood that Merriot's knuckles were scraped and bleeding.
It looked as though he had missed a regular turn-up. "I say,
what has been happening here? You know, Father, it looks
damned odd to me. What are you all doing in the middle of
nowhere in any case?"

"Why, you ungrateful young puppy!" fumed his father.
"What do you suppose we are doing!"

"We, or rather I, was looking for Emily. Your father was
kind enough to assist me. That is all, Simon," answered Eleanor
wearily, for she was beginning to feel quite faint again.

"Yes, but... well, why are you here, Lord Merriot?" pursued Simon.

"I also came to... er... assist. Have you any objection?"
drawled his lordship with studied hauteur.

"No, not the least in the world. I just thought it was a
little..."

"Odd? Yes, so you said before. I assure you that the situation
appears no more peculiar to you than your somewhat strange

elopement appears to me. I must cultivate Miss Emily's acquaintance. She seems to be a damsel of unusual enterprise."

Simon was beginning to look a little ugly. Eleanor judged it time to intervene. "My dear boy, would you please stop asking foolish questions upon matters which do not concern you in the least and hand me into that coach. I must get back to London as soon as possible."

"Of course, ma'am." Mr. Trafford bowed, offering his hand. "Shall I see you at home, Father?"

"Naturally," replied that gentleman curtly.

Eleanor was conscious of Merriot at her side. "My dear, wait," he urged in a low tone.

"I am sorry, my lord, there is nothing to wait for," she answered sadly, and turning her back on his beloved countenance she stepped into the chaise.

The coach went bowling on its way, leaving two gentlemen looking after it.

"Lennox!" suddenly said Merriot.

"Yes?"

"What a couple of gulls we look, running after a female who will have nothing to do with either of us! Why don't we go inside and split a bottle!"

"A damned good notion, sir," answered Lennox, holding out a hand to his late opponent. "I'll drink to your health."

"And I to yours. Damn it, if she will have neither of us, what is to stop us?"

They turned with one accord into the taproom and shocked the worthy landlord by consuming by far the greater portion of his finest brandy.

Eleanor, meanwhile, being jolted at high speed along the highway, was conscious of being a good deal more sickly than mere fatigue warranted. Her head ached, her nose was stuffy and her throat was prickly and sore. By the time the chaise reached London she was running a high fever and was able, without consulting a physician, to diagnose her complaint. She had caught a dreadful cold!

The first person to meet her as she entered the house was Lord Portland, considerably put out and more worried than he liked to appear. "Eleanor, where have you been?" he demanded angrily. "And where is my daughter?"

"She is quite safe, brother, I promise you. She ran off with young Trafford, but it is all right. He took her to his aunt's house. She is there now."

Lord Portland was understandably bewildered. "But why on earth should she have run away with the young man? I would have had no objection to the match. None in the world!"

"Unfortunately, Lord Lennox did not take your attitude; he objected most strongly."

Lord Portland became quite red in the face. "That fellow has the audacity to object to my daughter?" he cried.

"No, Peter, merely to her aunt," interposed Eleanor calmly.

"Well, if that is the case why were you chasing all over the country with the man? The servants tell me you were seen leaving with him yesterday. Have you been with him all this time?"

"I had to have help in finding Emily. As Simon's father it seemed natural to ask him."

"Lennox! Have you no sense at all, Eleanor? Do you not know that if this gets out you will be ruined for good!" shouted his lordship in exasperation.

"I have not given the matter much thought, Peter, but I daresay you are right. At the moment I do not very much care. I am going to bed."

"A fine time to be going off to bed! Would it be asking too much to know where exactly I may find my daughter?" demanded Lord Portland sarcastically.

She gave a shaky little laugh. "Do you know, I quite forgot to ask. Simon will know. I should ask him."

"Upon my word, ma'am, you are mighty cool!" spluttered her brother. Then he realized that huge tears were pouring silently down his sister's averted cheek. In an instant his anger died and he laid his arm about her shoulder.

"My dear, has it been very hard?" he asked gently.

His kindness overcame her resolution; she turned in his comforting arms and, laying her head upon his shoulder, she cried just as she had when she was a small girl and had brought her childish griefs to her big brother. "There, there," he murmured, patting her head. "There, there. We will make it all right again. I will not let anything happen to you. The servants will not talk, I will make sure of that. Come, my dear, I am not angry with you anymore."

"Dear Peter, how good you are to me," she said gratefully. "But I do feel so very ill. I must go up to bed." He laid his hand upon her forehead and exclaimed in dismay, "Good heavens, girl, you are burning up. Go along with you at once. I shall send for the doctor immediately!"

Eleanor trailed slowly up the stairs, almost thankful that her physical ills prevented her from dwelling too much upon her misery. While her head was aching so, she could not think too much about Merriot, and that was a blessing. Dimly she knew that she was the most miserable creature alive, but as she sank back against the feather pillows and sipped the hot lemon and honey that her abigail had brought her, she was conscious only of a deep desire to sleep.

No doubt it was because she was overtired and unhappy that Eleanor had so little strength to fight her illness. There was a great fear that the chill might descend to her lungs and for several days the household servants went about their tasks as silently as possible. However concerned they were with their young mistress, they were not above spreading the gossip among the other servants in the neighborhood. Within a few hours every lady of fashion was aware that Eleanor Portland was dying and the news was discussed with as much relish in the salons as in the servants' halls. This was how Lady Jersey came to hear of it. She was very much shocked and at once ordered her carriage. While on her way to South Audley Street she chanced to see a gentleman walking down Piccadilly.

"Merriot!" she called. "Merriot, is there any news?"

"News, Lady Jersey? News of what?" he asked rather impatiently.

"Why, of poor Eleanor, of course. I thought you would know more than the rest of us. They say it is likely to enter her lungs."

He fixed his eyes upon her with painful intensity. "What is this? Is Eleanor ill?"

"Good heavens, did you not know it then?"

"I have but this morning returned to town. Tell me, for God's sake. What is wrong with Eleanor?"

"I am sorry, I would not for the world . . . I am sure it cannot be as bad as they say," stammered Lady Jersey, for once startled out of her poise.

"And just what is it they do say?" he asked with deceptive calm.

"Why, that the poor child caught the most dreadful cold and that it has quite brought her down. An inflammation of the lungs is feared by all accounts. The child must have been weaker than she seemed, for I had always thought her the very picture of health. However, I have known a mere chill to carry off a man in his prime. There is no telling with such things."

"My God, ma'am, every word you speak is torture!" he cried out suddenly. "I must go to her!"

"Merriot, be calm. The sickroom is no place for you. I doubt very much if you would be allowed to see her, and if you did very likely you would simply upset the poor thing for no good reason. We must not allow her to suffer a relapse. I am on my way there now, and I shall send you word as soon as I have seen her. Do not worry, my dear friend. She will be well directly, I am convinced."

When Lady Jersey arrived at the house she was surprised to find the household going about its business in very much the usual way. There was no straw spread outside in the street nor were the servants making any attempt to go silently about their business. In short, this hardly seemed like a house of sickness, and she was greatly cheered.

"Is Miss Portland well enough to receive visitors?" she demanded of Fiskin, who was bowing deferentially before her.

"I shall inquire, my lady, if you would care to wait in the morning room. Miss is still delicate but improving, I am happy to say."

A few minutes later Lady Jersey was embracing her friend, tears swimming in her sharp gray eyes. "My dear, you are quite wasted away!" she exclaimed.

"I have not been able to eat very much," admitted Eleanor. "But I think that my appetite is coming back a little. Is it not ridiculous to be so pulled down by a cold? I swear I thought I was going to die!"

"Why, so did everyone else, my dear! It is too silly, but the rumor has been flying around the town that you are at death's door. I cannot think how such a thing happened, but really, everyone is so concerned. I shall be able to reassure them. You will be getting a lot of visitors now it is known that you are well enough to receive them."

Eleanor sighed. "People are very kind. I have had so many lovely flowers sent to me." She did not add that the one card she had been hoping for had been absent. Merriot had sent nothing.

"Tell me, my dear, is it true that little Emily is to be

married?" asked Lady Jersey. "I could scarcely believe it when I was told that she was going to marry young Trafford. Not that there is anything against the match. I should say it was very suitable if it were not for . . . Well, it must be very embarrassing for you, my love!"

"A little, dear ma'am, I must admit, but now I am grown accustomed to the notion. Poor Emily, it would have been so unkind to have thrown difficulties in her way," answered Eleanor airily. She wondered if any rumor of the elopement had reached Lady Jersey. Apparently not. Eleanor could not but be thankful. Kind though her old friend might be, gossip was the essence of life to her and such a juicy morsel would not be kept to herself.

After perhaps half an hour Lady Jersey jumped up in her restless way and informed the invalid that she must be off. "For I have to tell a certain gentleman who was most anxious about you that we were needlessly alarmed. He will be excessively relieved, I can tell you!" She smiled and patted Eleanor's cheek. "What a sly little thing you are, to be sure."

Eleanor longed to know which particular gentleman Lady Jersey was referring to, but she was too proud to ask. If Merriot wished to inquire about her he could come to the house, as had so many other gentlemen. Why, even the Reverend Higginbottom had called. Not to mention Mr. Osborne, Lord Byron, Mr. Brummell, and Prime Minister himself. Indeed, if she had not been so very miserable she would have been overcome by the attention she had received.

Within a day or two she was sufficiently recovered to allow herself to be dressed and to spend the day in sitting by a cozy fire reading or engaging in her exquisite embroidery. She was looking forward to her niece's return at the end of the week for she was in need of company and so was grateful when Harriet, having summoned up the courage to face her again, paid her a call.

"Can you forgive me?" she asked timidly upon first being admitted into Eleanor's presence.

Eleanor opened her arms to the child and hugged her warmly. "It is I who should ask for forgiveness. I was quite horrid to you and you bore it like an angel. What is more, it is entirely due to you that my reputation is not in shreds. If you had not spread the tale about that Emily and I were away visiting Simon's relatives then I do not know where we should have been!"

"I did my best, ma'am," averred Harriet. "I thought it best to tell just a few of Lady Radcliff's friends, in strictest confidence. I knew they would spread the story, for I never met such a set of nasty old gossips in my life!"

"Well done, Harriet. I have underestimated you," laughed Eleanor.

"I am glad that Emily and Simon will be getting married in the normal way after all. I am sure it is very romantic to elope, but I have always thought that it must be excessively uncomfortable!"

Eleanor laughed again. "Indeed it is, my dear. What a sensible child you are!"

"Well, I should not like to have to do without a wedding dress and bridesmaids. One only gets married once after all."

"Let us hope so in any event," teased Eleanor.

"Oh, I know I could never love anyone but Frederick. When one truly loves someone, one can never change," stated Harriet confidently.

Eleanor gave a little sigh. "That is not quite true. It is possible to fall in love again, but it is not always as happy an experience as the first time."

Harriet, sensing that she had in some way distressed her hostess, immediately began chattering about her wedding. When Eleanor was alone, however, her mind returned to its accustomed path. Where was Merriot? Why did he not come to her? What had gone wrong with their love, and was it perhaps her fault? There were no answers to these questions, but still they revolved in her head until she thought that she was going mad.

When Lady Jersey sent a note to Merriot, reassuring him and reporting the true state of affairs, he experienced a relief and gratitude so profound that it startled him. Although Eleanor had been in no real danger he felt as though she had been saved in order that they might have a second chance together. He resolved once more to offer her his love and this time there would be no turning back. They belonged together and he knew it. He resolved to wait until she was completely well before making his move and began instead putting his house in order.

Weston, upon receiving a great many orders to do with

household management, a matter with which his lordship had never previously concerned himself, went so far as to ask his lordship if he was contemplating a change.

"If you will forgive my asking, sir, is there going to be a lady in the house?"

"There is indeed, Weston, and I want the place fit to receive her. Engage any more staff that you think we shall require and have the blue room fitted up as a boudoir."

"Certainly, sir. May I ask the lady's name?" asked the man discreetly.

Merriot, however, thought it would be as well to keep that information to himself. Weston was not the man to prate about his master's concerns, but there were other servants, no less observant, who were far from reticent and soon set the word about town that their master was to marry.

Lord Portland, entering the sacred portals of White's Club, was surprised to find himself hailed by a gentleman he scarcely knew but whom he was aware had the reputation of being an inveterate scandalmonger. He could not conceive what Mr. Byng should want with him, but he politely stopped and waited until he should come up with him.

"I say, Portland, I wanted to be the the first to congratulate you," said Mr. Byng, holding out his hand.

"Thank you, sir," answered his lordship politely. "I am very pleased with the match, I must admit."

"I should think so indeed," responded Mr. Byng warmly. "It will be the wedding of the season, no doubt about that."

Lord Portland was surprised. "I had not thought of it in that way, I must confess. They are both very young and..." He broke off, for his interlocutor had burst into shrieks of laughter. "Very young! Oh, but that is rich...damn it, that is funny. I did not know that you were a wit, sir."

Lord Portland drew himself up, offended by this unseemly mirth. "I do not understand what you find so amusing about my daughter's youth, sir!"

The laughter stopped instantly. "Oh, I beg pardon, sir! I did not know that you were referring to Miss Emily. We have been at cross purposes. I would not for the world have given offense."

"To whom else could I have been referring?" demanded Lord Portland in exasperation.

"Why, to Miss Portland and Merriot. I thought that you were making a joke," explained Mr. Byng with an inane laugh.

His lordship was thunderstruck. "I have not the faintest idea what you are talking about, Byng. My sister is not about to be married. That I can assure you."

"But it is all over town that Merriot is to put his head in the noose at last and, of course, everyone believed . . . Well, their partiality for one another has been marked. No offense now, Portland, but you cannot deny that it has been marked."

"I would be most grateful, sir, if you would negate this particular rumor whenever you chance to hear it. My sister has contracted no engagement that I know of. What is more, she would do nothing without consulting my wishes."

"Oh, of course, of course," cried Mr. Byng. "Only too happy. But what puzzles me is, if it is not Miss Portland, then who is it?"

"I neither know nor care!" snapped his lordship and stalked into the club. Mr. Byng was by no means the only gentleman to mention the matter to him that day, and to each he gave the same answer. However, in the face of such a strong rumor he began to have doubts himself and upon returning to the house the first thing he did was seek out his sister and confront her with the story.

"Eleanor! Eleanor! Here's a damn thing!" he called as he entered the drawing room.

"Good heavens, Peter, must you make so much noise?" asked Eleanor, who had jumped nervously at the sudden sound.

"Well, my girl, I hope you are satisfied. You have succeeded in making yourself the talk of the town once more. Do you know that it's all over the clubs that Merriot is to be married and that you, *you* are to be his bride?"

She grew pale. "Merriot is to marry?" she repeated falteringly.

"Aye, so they say. He may be for all I care. What bothers me is that everyone seems to think that you are to be his wife!"

"No brother. It is not I," she answered him.

"Then might I ask what has been going on in my absence to lead impertinent persons to assume that it is indeed yourself that Merriot intends to marry?"

Eleanor hesitated, but felt that no good could come of attempting to deceive her brother. Haltingly she told him the whole story, omitting only that precious night they had spent together. Lord Portland was fond of his sister and was really grieved that she should be so unhappy. When he heard, however, that she had also declined offers from Mr. Osborne and Lord Lennox he began to feel that she could manage very well without his sympathy. "Upon my word, Eleanor, I had hoped that you might perhaps receive an eligible offer if you were to come to London, but this is incredible. Do you really mean to tell me that Lennox is willing to divorce his wife in order to marry you?"

"That is what he said, Peter," she replied.

"And that you received a declaration from Osborne and refused him?"

"I did, brother. I could not have been the kind of wife he needs."

"Well, my dear, I am no advocate of marriage between two people who dislike each other, but to be whistling down the wind a fortune of over a hundred thousand simply because of a romantic scruple . . . Well, well, I will say no more. Since you have half the gentlemen in London at your feet no doubt you will have other offers. They say Clarence is hanging out for a wife," Lord Portland said sarcastically.

Eleanor, however, declined to consider the Regent's portly brother and once more declared her fixed intention of remaining single.

"Well, I will not deny that I shall be glad to have you back at Hawthorne, but reflect how very awkward your position in my house will be once Emily is married. Let us not deceive ourselves. I cannot protect you from Maria all the time, and if you return to us you will become nothing more than an unpaid companion and nurse. My dear, I am too fond of you to wish that to happen. Why not reconsider Osborne's offer?"

"Say no more, I beg of you!" exclaimed Eleanor. "Do you think that I have not considered all that you say? I have not told you all! I can marry no one else now. Understand me please and say no more!"

Some inkling of the truth dawned upon Lord Portland. He patted her hand, compassion in his kindly eyes. "Well, my dear, something may yet happen to set all right. Do not despair."

chapter 15

Eleanor did make a determined effort to be cheerful, not because she believed her brother's words but because she knew her gloomy presence put a blight upon the whole household. She found it difficult to support her spirits when alone, however, and so it was with real delight that she welcomed Emily home that evening.

It was the sound of a post chaise drawing up outside the house that first alerted her to her niece's arrival. She sprang up hastily, easy tears filling her eyes. When Emily, with some trepidation, entered the room, Eleanor flung her arms around her and held her close.

"Dear Aunt Eleanor, I was so afraid that you would be angry with me," disclosed Emily shyly. "Simon has told me how you came after us and how it made you so ill. I never thought that I would put you to so much trouble!"

Eleanor gave a shaky laugh. "That is one way of putting it! My dear, I had to do what I could. How were you to know what damage your flight could have done to you and to your future happiness? I felt that I had a duty to prevent you from ruin if I could. Of course, I see now that I should have trusted

Simon. He would never allow any harm to come to you." The unspoken thought was that Simon differed from his father in this respect, but neither lady made any comment. Instead Eleanor drew her niece toward the cozy fire and urged her to tell her part of the story.

"Well, I must say that at first I thought that Simon had played me an excessively shabby trick. For a long time I did not notice anything amiss. It was dark and I could not see where we were going. But then we turned into the gates of a big house, I could see the lodges and I began to be afraid that Simon intended to . . . that perhaps he did not really mean to marry me after all. However, Aunt Letty—she asked me to call her that—was there to greet us, and I knew at once that it was all right. She was so kind in explaining to me that I could not marry Simon in such a scrambling way. She is the Viscount's aunt, you know, and he is very fond of her. She said that I could stay with her until she had persuaded him to change his mind and allow us to marry. Of course, then I was quite happy not to go to Gretna, for I will be able to have just the kind of wedding I wanted now!"

"So you expect me to pay for an extravagant wedding, do you, Puss?" came her father's voice from the doorway. "After all the trouble you have caused?"

"Papa!" cried Emily, running to him. "Oh, Papa, I have missed you so much!"

Any words of censure that his lordship had been intending to speak remained unuttered. He took his errant daughter in his arms and kissed her heartily. Then he held her at arm's length and inspected her, laughing at her changed appearance.

"Why, what has happened to my little girl? Suddenly you are quite grown up!"

"Oh, it is only that I have put up my hair in a new mode. Do you like it?" she answered airily.

"No, it is more than that. You have changed, my little one," he said rather sadly.

Eleanor smiled. "It is a natural change, Peter. You would not have Emily remain a child forever."

"No. No, I suppose I would not. I only hope young Trafford realizes what a wife he is getting. He should be grateful."

Emily put her arm through his. "Of course he is, Papa. Simon loves me and I love him, very, very much."

"Then I am satisfied. Am I allowed to know when the

wedding is to take place?" said Lord Portland, attempting to hide his emotion behind his sarcasm.

"Silly, of course you are! I want to be married in June. I think that everything can be ready by then. Do not you, Aunt?"

"Certainly. June is the very best month for a wedding," she answered warmly.

"And when are you to be married, dearest Aunt?" questioned Emily innocently.

Eleanor had quite forgotten that when she had last seen Emily she had been very full of plans for her future with Merriot. It seemed cruel that she must be reminded of them now.

"I . . . I am not going to . . . to marry Lord Merriot after all, Emily," she managed to say in a quivering voice. "Excuse me a moment, if you please!" With that she fled from the room, her hand to her mouth to stifle her sobs.

"Good gracious, whatever has happened, Papa?" demanded Emily in astonishment. "Why, I had never seen her so happy before . . . and now . . . Something dreadful must have happened!"

Lord Portland nodded. "I do not pretend to understand the whole of it, my love. Your aunt is a remarkably proud woman and from what I can understand Merriot insulted her beyond all forgiveness. I agree that it is very unfortunate because from what I have seen I think Merriot the very man for her. He is in any event a far cry from that man milliner that she fell in love with before!" Lord Lennox was not a favorite with his lordship.

"Oh, but how silly!" cried Miss Emily, quite disgusted. "To allow a ridiculous thing like pride to keep her from him. Why, she adores the man!"

"Well, it seems as though she no longer has a choice. It appears that Lord Merriot is going to be married to some other lady," her father informed her.

"What? No, I do not believe it! Why, you have only to see how he looks at her. He would never marry anyone else. No, Papa, the whole thing is a stupid misunderstanding. We must help her!"

"My dear, I am sure I hope that you are right, but I know my sister. That pride of hers is all that she had to defend herself with for ten long years. She cannot change so easily."

Emily sighed. "Papa, how sad it would be if she has to

return to Pudsley for the rest of her life. She has changed since she came to London. She has grown so much more beautiful. Many gentlemen admire her, you know."

"Well, Puss, if you can talk some sense into her you have my blessing, but, frankly, I think it unlikely, for of all stiff-necked females she is the worst!"

Eleanor had sufficiently composed herself by the time that Emily scratched upon her door to call, "Come in," in a reasonably firm voice. Although she looked pale, all traces of tears had disappeared, and she was sitting by the fire attempting to read, although what the book was about she could no more have said than if it were written in Chinese.

"Dearest Aunt, may I come in?" asked Emily. Without waiting for an answer she closed the door behind her. Seeing how unhappy Eleanor looked she ran to her side and, sinking to the floor beside her chair, she took her hands and laid her cheek upon them. "Dearest Aunt, it is all my fault that you are so unhappy. If I had not run away . . ."

"Hush, my dear. I do not blame you. My eyes are opened to his real character, and I consider that I am very . . . very . . . fortunate . . . Oh, Emily!"

"Please, do not cry!" exclaimed Emily distressfully. "I am sure that all this can be untangled. Lord Merriot loves you dearly. I know he does!"

"So dearly that already he is planning to marry someone else. I have been so foolish, so wickedly foolish! I made sure that he would come to me to beg me to forgive him. He always has before. I was going to punish him a little and then forgive him . . . but instead I have heard nothing from him. He has not even sent me a posy of flowers!"

Emily considered. "Well, if he has always come to you before, then I think it only fair that this time you should go to him. After all, this story of his marriage cannot really be true. Why, only a few days ago he was betrothed to you. Where could he have found another bride so soon? It is probably just a rumor."

"Do you think so, indeed? Yes, you must be right. I have been so unhappy that I have not thought clearly upon the matter. Perhaps he will come yet!"

Emily shook her head. "No, Aunt. I believe that he is waiting for you to go to him. There is no room for pride when one loves. Simon has taught me that."

Eleanor bit her lip. "No . . . not that. I cannot. I will not be like all the other women who have clung to him long after he has ceased to care for them. I have heard how he regards them. I will not allow him to talk of me with such contempt."

Emily was defeated. There seemed nothing she could say to move Eleanor from this position.

Eleanor passed a miserable night, tossing and turning while her mind raced. At one moment she would decide to go to him, at another the memory of his words to her angered her so much that she wanted to hit him. She would not be just another woman in his life, even if it meant never seeing him again. If only she knew whether he really wanted her or not! Then she would not hesitate. When she thought of his tender lovemaking she could not but believe that he truly loved her, but why in that case had he been silent for so long?

"What am I to do?" she whispered desperately in the darkness. "What in God's name am I to do?"

The next morning she arose still pale and heavy-eyed. She had fallen asleep shortly before dawn, but as her rest had been disturbed by horrid dreams she awoke tense and fatigued.

Languidly she allowed herself to be arrayed in whatever her abigail, a pleasant girl but by no means as friendly as Lucy, put out for her. As this chanced to be a lavender dimity, much tucked about the bodice and with a scalloped hem, she still appeared very lovely and rather fragile.

Both her brother and her niece had a tendency to treat her as an invalid that morning. They waited upon her, tempting her appetite as best they could. She was touched and a little amused by this and did her best to gratify them by swallowing a few of the delicacies they offered.

"Do you know, Aunt, I would like to take a drive into the country today. Would you not like to come, too?" asked Emily, who normally would have voted such a drive the most boring thing in the world. "We could go to Richmond. Simon would be delighted to accompany us, I am sure."

"Thank you, sweetheart, but I really think that I would rather stay here for today. Indeed, it looks as though it might rain," answered Eleanor with a grateful smile.

"Oh, I do not think so. Do you, Papa?" demanded Emily eagerly.

"Frankly, my dear, I do not have the slightest notion. The sky is a little overcast certainly. Perhaps a drive is not a very good idea. You may always go another day."

"Well, I do not wish to stay indoors all day. Papa, may I have the carriage to take me to visit Harriet?" said Emily with the suggestion of a pout.

"Of course, my dear. I will order it to be brought round in half an hour."

"Thank you, Papa. Aunt Eleanor, would you like to come with me to see Harriet?" she asked, although without much expectation of a favorable reply.

The thought that she might perhaps meet Lady Radcliff there so appalled Eleanor that she declined this treat also and assured her anxious niece that she would really much rather spend the morning quietly with a book. Emily, who interpreted this to mean that she would spend the morning brooding, was reluctant to leave, but as she really did want to talk to Harriet she left her aunt and ran upstairs to put on her bonnet.

Eleanor had quite convinced herself that she had no expectation of ever seeing Lord Merriot again; nevertheless, as soon as she was alone she was on tenterhooks, listening for the sound of his coming. She jumped up at the sound of every carriage and ran to the window only to be disappointed.

When, after an hour or so of this, a carriage did eventually halt outside the house, she was in a state of such nervous prostration that she could only remain in her chair, silently praying that it would indeed be he.

"Viscount Lennox," announced Fiskin with a bow.

The disappointment was so intense that she felt that she had received a blow. However, that was no excuse, she believed, for ill breeding, and so she arose to greet his lordship with very creditable composure.

"Good day, my lord," she said in a tight little voice.

"Eleanor, I have longed to see you again," he told her, grasping her hand. "When I learned of your illness I was distraught!"

"I only had a cold, sir," she replied, not in the least gratified by this ardor. "Please have the goodness to let go of my hand."

He seemed discouraged. "Well, a cold can be a pretty serious thing. I have known cases . . . However, I did not come here to discuss such matters. Eleanor, I have to tell you that I have not been able to get you out of my mind these past days!"

"I am sorry for it, sir," she answered, regarding him composedly but without a hint of interest. He found it hard to continue under that cool scrutiny.

"Have you forgiven me yet for my stupid behavior that night? I have not been able to sleep for thinking of it. I deserve to be flogged!"

She looked a little puzzled. "Your behavior? Oh, yes. I am afraid I had forgotten about that," she told him truthfully. More painful considerations had quite driven it from her mind.

"Forgotten!" He seemed thunderstruck by this announcement. "How could anyone forget a thing like that? Upon my word I have been torturing myself all these days thinking that you must hate me and all the time you have forgotten all about it!"

He was so put out that she could not but smile a little. "But I thought that you wanted me to forgive you, Richard. I have forgiven and forgotten as a Christian should."

He seemed still inclined to take a pet. "I suppose the truth is that the entire incident mattered so little to you that you were able just to dismiss it from your mind. It is not so with me, I assure you!"

"I am sorry, Richard. I seem to have offended you. I did not mean to."

Her words recalled him to his mission. "Offended!" he cried. "How could I be offended with you, my dearest? You are my dream, my goddess!" He fell upon his knees before her. "I love you, Eleanor. You know that. Will you not give me some hope that I may win you back to me in time?"

She was reluctant to hurt him. "Richard, you are married. It is as impossible now as it ever was. Even if I still cared for you . . ."

"Do you? Do you care at all?" he asked, a little wistfully.

"How I feel does not enter into the matter, Richard."

"I am a fool. I have not told you the real reason that I am here. The sight of you put it out of my mind. Eleanor, Alyce has left me. She has run off with some young puppy half her age. I am compelled to divorce her. Honor demands it!"

"I am sorry to hear this, Richard. Simon will be made unhappy by it, I am afraid," she said seriously.

"Devil a bit! If you pardon the expression. There is little enough love lost between Simon and his mother. I do not think he has even seen her this age," responded Lord Lennox with a shrug.

"Then it seems that I must congratulate you rather than offering you my sympathy. I know it has not been very easy for you to be married to a woman of her kind!" she said with a smile.

He nodded. "It hurt like the devil at first, I must confess. It was your love that healed me. You who brought me back to life. Will you not come back to me now? There is no happiness for me without you."

He was watching her with painful intensity. She wondered how it was she could feel nothing for him, not even a mild fondness. She was not at all sure she even liked the man. Yet it was hard to say no and see that expression of hope die out of his eyes. Why must she who had been so desperately hurt now inflict pain upon others?

"Richard, it is too late," she said gently. "Had you come to me only a few weeks ago I believe I would have fallen into your arms. But that would have been a great mistake for both of us. You see, my dear, I do not believe you are truly in love with me. You are still in love with the girl you used to know. I am not the same person, Richard."

"To me you are!" he exclaimed. "The only difference I can see is that you are more lovely now than ever. I have changed, I know, but not in my love for you. That is as strong as ever!"

"So strong that you lived perfectly happily without me for ten years?" she replied, beginning to be angry. "I think you only began to think of me again when you realized I was sought after by other men. The truth of the matter is simple jealousy."

"You cannot believe it! I will not deny the sight of you and Merriot drove me near frantic, but that was only after my love had reanimated toward you. I could see you were in love with him, but I hoped after the scene the other day you might have recovered from your infatuation."

"How dare you! What I feel for Merriot is no infatuation. I have never loved anyone . . . anyone, Lennox, as I do him."

"Then where is he?" demanded his lordship, who was fast losing control over his temper. "And does he know the full story about us? Have you dared to tell him about the night we spent together?"

"Merriot knows everything there is to know about it. We

have both put it out of our minds for good. He knows there is no need to be jealous of the past!"

"You might have spared me." said Lennox quietly. "You are very cruel, my dear."

"I beg your pardon." she answered in a mortified tone. "Perhaps it would be better if you were to go now before either of us says any more to hurt the other. We shall meet at Emily's wedding. By that time I hope we shall both have recovered ourselves enough to meet with complaisance."

He bowed and walked slowly to the door as though hoping to hear her voice calling him back. She did not call. He turned as he opened the door and saw her standing by the window looking out, a faraway expression in her lovely eyes. She had forgotten him already.

chapter 16

Eleanor did not even notice the unfortunate Viscount's departure. She was listening to her own words ringing in her ears, exulting in the memory. How could she have doubted their love for a moment? She had been proud to avow it to the man before her; there was nothing to prevent her from making the same avowal to her lover, nothing except her own foolish pride. But pride was a luxury she could no longer afford. She had waited for him and he had not come. Very well, she would go to him . . . now!

She gave herself no time to think nor to doubt but hurried up the stairs to her chamber where, without so much as a glance in the mirror, she tied on her bonnet, donned a pelisse, and fairly ran out of the house.

The jarvey who took her up seemed dubious about taking a lady into St. James in broad daylight, for although he was quite accustomed to driving a certain sort of female to this haunt of bachelors, he had never driven an unescorted lady of quality there before.

But a disappointment awaited Eleanor when she eventually arrived at Lord Merriot's door. His lordship was not at home and his manservant had not the slightest idea when he would return.

Eleanor took a deep breath and resolutely announced her intention of awaiting his lordship. "Lord Merriot will not object, I assure you," she told the man in a firm voice.

Weston, who had become something of a connoisseur in the years in which he had served his lordship, was inclined to agree. No sane man, in his opinion, could possibly object to finding this radiant vision awaiting him at home. She was not his usual type and Weston personally found the voluptuous Amanda more to his taste, but there was no doubt that she was a diamond of the very first water.

It never occurred to the man that he might be confronting his master's future wife. A respectable woman did not call unaccompanied upon a bachelor and there was no doubt in Weston's mind that the future Lady Merriot would be the essence of respectability. Merriot might be a little lax but his lady would be above reproach, of that Weston was sure.

Eleanor had caught the man's appraising look and it had cut her to the quick. Almost she left the house, but then she took herself to task. The man was not to be blamed for what he so obviously believed; indeed, he had every reason to think ill of her. She was not the first woman to visit Merriot, she supposed. The thought pained her almost unbearably. She could not go on like this, she told herself. If she was to suffer every time someone or something reminded her that she was not the first woman in her lover's life then there would be no happiness for her nor for him. She must learn to accept the truth he had told her about himself just as he had accepted her. All the many difficulties they had in the course of their relationship had been caused through a lack of trust upon both their parts. She determined that she, at least, would cease to suspect an infidelity every time a woman from Merriot's past appeared.

So she sat in his lordship's library with every appearance of composure and, if she did not go so far as to order Weston to bring her a bottle of wine, she did request him to bring her the tea tray.

Lord Merriot, quite unconscious of the happiness awaiting him, was strolling along Pall Mall en route to his club when he chanced to see Viscount Lennox walking toward him.

"Lennox, well met, sir!" called Lord Merriot in a good-humored tone. "When did you get back to town?"

The Viscount, having departed from his lordship upon friendly terms, could hardly return to his former manner without giving offense, and so he answered warmly enough. "Good day, Merriot. I have been back several days now. And yourself?"

"Oh, a couple of days ago. I went up to my lodge in Leicestershire after I left you. I wanted to have a look at the yearlings. Are you on your way to the club?"

"I had thought of looking in," acknowledged Lennox.

"Then would you care for a hand of piquet, sir?" asked Merriot, who was anxious to find out if Lord Lennox had seen Miss Portland and if so with what result.

Lennox shrugged. "Certainly, Merriot," he answered. As it was still early there were few gentlemen in the gaming rooms at Watier's and they were able to find a table easily enough. Merriot ordered the waiter to bring them a bottle of claret and a fresh deck of cards. Neither man was in a very talkative mood, but they did exchange a few remarks.

"I believe the wedding is to be next month?" said Merriot, expertly dealing the cards. "Mr. Trafford must be delighted with the way things have turned out."

"My son is happy enough, I believe. It will be a very small affair now, of course. It would scarcely be fitting to have a large formal wedding under the circumstances."

"The circumstances?" queried his lordship, scanning his hand absently.

"You have not heard, sir? I had thought it would be all over town by now."

"I assure you, Lennox, I have not the slightest idea what you are referring to," Merriot assured him, wondering if these circumstances had anything to do with Eleanor.

"Why, sir, I see no reason to keep the thing a secret. If I do not tell you, no doubt some other busybody soon will. The fact of the matter is that my wife has run off with one Captain Renwick of the Guards," said Lennox, without noticeable distress.

"I beg your pardon, Lennox. I had no idea!" exclaimed Merriot. He fell silent thinking that this might very well affect the way in which Eleanor regarded the Viscount's proposal. While she might shrink from being the cause of his divorce, she could not have any moral objection to marrying a man deserted by a faithless wife. He frowned, wondering how best he could broach the subject.

"Since you were good enough to confide in me that you proposed to divorce Lady Lennox in any event, I shall not condole with you. I should be most grateful, however, if you would be kind enough to tell me what your plans are regarding the future."

"I think you really mean in regard to Eleanor, do you not, Merriot?" said Lennox with a wry smile.

"As you say, sir."

"Do not concern yourself, my lord, you are quite safe," Lennox told him.

"You mean that you are no longer a suitor for her hand?" asked Merriot, watching his opponent closely.

"Not at all. I mean that I have already asked Eleanor to do me the honor of becoming my wife and have been rejected in terms that leave no room for continued hope."

"She knows that you will be free to marry her honorably and she still refused you?" exclaimed Merriot eagerly.

"My lord, she has no feelings for me or for anyone but yourself. If you do not know that then you are a fool!" said the Viscount in some exasperation.

Merriot was too delighted with this information to resent the way in which it was given. "She told you that?"

"Yes, she did. I cannot say that I am exactly happy for you, Merriot, but I wish you both well. It was too late, far too late for us, even if she had been willing." He sighed and shook his head. "Eleanor is not the same girl that I have remembered all these years. No doubt she is a stronger and perhaps a finer person, but I cannot help remembering her as she once was, so trusting, so vulnerable! What a pity she had to change!"

"I cannot agree with you, sir, but I am delighted that you feel that way. You have relieved my mind greatly. Now, shall we play?"

The game lasted well into the afternoon; it was past six o'clock when Lord Merriot, richer by several hundred guineas, at last arrived home.

"My lord! Thank goodness you have come home!" exclaimed Weston, in some relief, when he opened the door to his lordship.

"This devotion is touching," remarked Merriot. "Is there any particular reason for it?"

"Yes, indeed, sir. There is a lady here to see you. She has been here for the best part of the afternoon. I did not know what was best to be done!"

"Not Lady Amanda?" sighed Merriot wearily, wondering how much it would cost him to get rid of her this time.

"No, indeed, my lord. I have never seen this lady before. She gave her name as Miss Portland, sir," answered the man.

"Eleanor! Here? Good God, man, why did you not send someone after me?" cried his lordship. "No, never mind your excuses. Where is she?"

"The lady is awaiting your lordship in the library," answered the man with an air of offended dignity.

Merriot strode across the hallway and flung open the door eagerly. Eleanor, tired out by the nervous storms of the past week and bored with waiting, had stretched herself upon his lordship's sofa and fallen asleep. She was lying in a far from seductive attitude, her mouth a little open, her lovely hair disheveled. He stood for a while looking down at her, the tenderest smile playing around his mouth. "Eleanor," he called softly. "Wake up, my dear."

"Robert?" she murmured sleepily. Her eyes fluttered open. "Robert!" she said again in a very different voice. "Oh, I did not mean to fall asleep. You must think me an idiot!"

At that he laughed. "Hardly that, my darling, but perhaps a little unwise. Why have you come here? It is not at all the thing."

She sat up abruptly. "Well, what else could I do? You would not come to me, although I waited and waited!"

He turned his head to hide a smile of triumph. In a cool voice he answered her. "But, my dear, I thought that I was behaving as you wished me to behave. You told me when last we met that you never wished to see me again. Do you not remember?"

"Of course I remember, but you should have known that I did not mean it, Merriot!" she cried hotly.

Then he showed her his laughing face. "Oh, my sweet darling. Of course I did. I was coming to you tonight!"

"Oh, you . . . you . . . Merriot!" she cried as he took her in his arms. "My darling, I am glad that I did not wait for you to come to me. I owed you this."

His arms tightened around her and his lips drew close to

hers. Just at that moment Weston once more appeared in the doorway.

"Lord Portland," he announced. The lovers exchanged startled glances as his lordship strode into the room.

Lord Portland was in no very good mood. He had returned home from a particularly tedious session in the House, only to find that his sister had once more disappeared. Neither Emily nor any of the servants had the smallest idea where she might have gone, but Hugo, that observant footman, offered that he had seen Miss depart in a hackney coach several hours earlier. He had not, unfortunately, been able to hear what direction she gave the driver.

Portland's first thought was that she had, for some reason, gone to Viscount Lennox. He had called upon that gentleman and been speedily convinced that he had no more idea where she was than her affectionate brother. He had, however, suggested that Lord Portland pay a call upon Lord Merriot. He had been inclined to dismiss this idea, knowing how unlikely it was that Eleanor, who had been so vehement in her refusal to send for Merriot, would have gone to him instead. However, he could look in on his lordship, there could be no harm in that. Nothing could have exceeded his surprise when upon inquiring of the manservant whether Miss Portland had been to the house, he was ushered into the library.

"Upon my word, Eleanor! Have you no discretion? Careless of your reputation I know you to be, but this! To be alone with a man at this hour...! Well, I have had enough. My lord, as this lady's brother, I demand to know what your intentions are!"

Merriot grinned. "Mostly, if not entirely, honorable," he answered.

"That is no answer. Do you mean marriage?" pursued Lord Portland, by no means satisfied with this reply.

"Really, Peter, this has nothing to do with you," interposed Eleanor rather crossly. "I am of age and my marriage is no concern of yours. I am no longer your ward."

"No, but you are my sister. What is more, you bear my name, and I will not have you bringing further disgrace upon it. You seem to be incapable of distinguishing between an honorable man and a scoundrel. It is up to me to see you are not imposed upon again!"

"If that is to my account I should like to know what you mean by calling me a scoundrel!" began Merriot angrily.

"Hush, darling," begged Eleanor. "Let us have no more quarreling. After all, Peter is quite right. I have brought disgrace upon the name and he has a perfect right to protect it if he can."

Lord Portland was furious. "To hell with the name! Can you not see it is you I am thinking of, Eleanor? I do not want you to suffer more than you have already. Good God, the whole world knows the man is to be married and yet I find you alone with him here. He can mean you nothing but harm!"

Lord Merriot seemed puzzled. "What in God's name are you talking about, Portland?" he demanded.

"Do not try to fool me. At least a dozen men have told me you are going to be married. What would the lady think if she knew you were entertaining my sister like this?"

"Why, you fool, who should I be going to marry but Eleanor?" cried Merriot in exasperation.

Lord Portland looked somewhat taken aback. "Well, if this is so perhaps you will explain why it was that Eleanor had no idea at all of your intentions when I spoke to her yesterday?"

"Peter, what does it matter?" interrupted Eleanor with a happy smile. "I should have trusted Lord Merriot as he has trusted me. It is all my fault. I should have known. Will you forgive me, my darling?"

He smiled at her in a way that made Lord Portland acutely embarrassed. "Of course I forgive you, my love. But nevertheless your brother is right. You should not be here. You must go home with him now and I will come to you tomorrow, I promise."

Eleanor was a little disappointed that their tender reconciliation scene should have been cut so short, but she had to submit to the two determined men who loved her.

"Oh, very well. But, Peter, you must leave us alone for a few minutes. There are some things I have to say to Lord Merriot before I go."

"I will await you in the carriage," replied her brother in disapproving accents. "I beg you will not be too long."

The two lovers were left alone together, a little uncertain of each other. They were silent for a few moments, then Eleanor lifted her head and met his eyes.

"Robert, I cannot leave without saying the things I came here to say. My darling, it was all my fault . . ."

"No," he interposed swiftly. "I was stupid . . . crass . . ."

"It was my fault, darling, and we both know it," she insisted firmly. "I told myself your way of life disgusted me. That I could not face marriage to a rake."

"They say a reformed rake makes the best husband," interpolated Merriot with a grin.

"I certainly hope so," she responded with a twinkle. "But what I meant to say was I have realized it was not disgust at your morals that upset me but simple, wicked jealousy. I could not bear to think of you making love to any other woman. I was even jealous of the women in your past. I cannot tell you what I suffered when I saw you in Amanda's arms."

"My dear, you know you will never have to worry . . ."

"Yes, I know, but I wish to make you a pledge. I promise you this, my darling. If I should come upon you in the arms of a dozen half-naked females, I will trust you and believe there is some simple and innocent explanation."

He laughed as he took her in his arms. "Eleanor, dearest Eleanor. I will make you a promise also. If I should happen to find you, miles from anywhere, having spent the night in the company of some distinguished gentleman, then I will believe with all my heart that if the worst came to the worst you would have hit him with a poker. Now, enough of all this. Kiss me good-bye, my darling, for you have to go soon."

She smiled up at him, her eyes glinting under half-closed lids.

"How very inconvenient of Peter to come looking for me. I could have stayed . . . a little longer," she murmured.

"Eleanor, you are quite shameless," he murmured, as his lips touched hers. "Thank God!"

In the carriage outside Lord Portland grew quite tired of waiting and with a shrug he ordered the coachman to take him home. They heard him depart and laughed a little guiltily. "I am afraid Peter will be very angry," she whispered as Merriot lifted her in his arms and carried her to the sofa.

He took her hand and held the palm to his lips. "Do you not understand yet, my little love? You will never have to care what anyone thinks of you or your conduct, ever again. You will be my wife."

"Robert, I will try to make you happy. To be the kind of wife you want," she sighed as he caressed her lovingly.

"You little fool, I am happier now than I have ever been before in my life. You are exactly the kind of wife I want," he told her tenderly.

With a little sigh of pure happiness she surrendered her lips to his. "I love you, I love you . . . I love you," were the last words she spoke for a very long time.